GREEN HOLLOW

GREEN
HOLLOW

G.S. HOWIE

Green Hollow
G.S. Howie

Table of Contents

Prologue

It could have been that Mr. Henry Winkler's decision to walk into the woods that night was based on a combination of curiosity and stubbornness. He was stubborn because he could not accept that what he was seeing was real. He was curious because he had never heard a song so beautiful and calming. It made his legs feel lighter as he walked through the moonlit woods. The forest stood thick with tall oaks and cypresses towering over his balding head.

Mr. Winkler was a practical man who refused the notion of things that went beyond the realm of what was natural. This was despite the stories told about his little town of Green Hollow. Ancient folk tales that Henry would scoff at and turn his nose up at whenever he heard them from one of the locals. He had hoped that the song that had lured him into the thickest part of the woods would be explained away. But why was he even doing this? Why did it feel as if his legs were moving without his consent? How had he even ended up here? Bits and pieces of memories came back as his legs continued marching forward ahead of him.

His car had broken down. He had been fighting with the engine. Something made him stop what he was doing and walk into the wood line despite the freezing cold that burned his ears and fingertips. But now he felt nothing. Only calm. He walked further and further into the branch-filled abyss. No animal made a sound. There were no bugs or birds; only that soft and haunting song could be heard.

Mr. Winkler reached a clearing. Giant rocks stood in a circle in the middle of it. From a distance, he could make out the silhouette of a woman dressed in a white gown. She was swaying. Something inside him felt unsettled by the woman in white's appearance. The closer Henry walked toward her, the more of her features he could make out. He realized she was incredibly tall and of fair complexion, so fair it seemed as if she was glowing. However, Mr. Winkler convinced himself it was simply a trick of the full moon above their heads. The woman in white stopped her dancing and stood as still as the surrounding rocks.

Mr. Winkler kept walking closer until he could make out more of her features. It was then that a deep sense of panic surged into his body, and though he urged it to allow him control again, it would not budge. He was firmly committed to moving toward the fair woman who had long fingers that were bone white with sharp-looking nails protruding from them. Her face seemed normal except for the occasional flashing images of flesh and bone. Henry was in front of her. He still had no control over his body, and his mind screamed for escape from what was about to happen. The cold white figure halted her song to stare into Henry's eyes. Her eyes were scarlet red. For a moment, there was only silence, a moment of intense quiet between the two figures. Then she opened her mouth, and what came out was an ear-piercing screech that brought him to his knees. He screamed, his ears bleeding and his mind feeling as though it was frying.

He fell dead.

Chapter 1

Miguel was never one to plan much in life. He went to college and changed his major three times before dropping out and becoming a food critic. He once got on the wrong flight and found himself in New York, only to rent an apartment a week later and never leave. Even his relationship with Benji started off with peanuts and an emergency room visit. But to find himself in a minivan, which the car dealer assured Benji they absolutely needed, with three kids and a grandpa was downright unexpected.

"Click!" They were on their way to a new house in the countryside. He had never thought he would be so far away from civilization, surrounded by an ocean of pine, cedar, and sapling. Isn't sapling a tree? "Click!" He already missed the honking horns and distant voices overheard through their tiny apartment window. "Click!" He missed his friends. "Click!" His job. "Click!"

"Okay, Wyatt. Super cool, but maybe we should stop making mouth sounds for now," he said. He glanced back to see the boy waving his bright green dinosaur over the brace on his left leg. Emma, his daughter, was sleeping in a position that only a child could manage, and the oldest, Gideon, listened to music that he could only assume was a combination of trash can lids banging together and angry grunts.

He noticed how the three children, though genetically related, had vastly different features that gave them each a distinct look. Wyatt, the youngest with his curly, unruly red hair, resembled a young Benji except for the boy's green eyes. He was a small, thin child who seemed to be swallowed by his car seat. On the other hand, his sister, ten years old, had light brown hair that reached her shoulders. Her face was without freckles; however, a small scar marked the right side of her eyebrow. Gideon's dark brown hair, cut short on the sides and longer on the top, was common among teenagers. It was a noticeable contrast with his siblings, though he shared the same green eyes and freckles as Wyatt. Sitting in the back, Grandpa Emory was a slender old man with a head of gray hair and a worn expression on his face. He glared out the window as if the trees somehow offended him.

"You doing alright, Peanut?" Benji asked, placing a hand on top of Miguel's.

He turned from his husband and faced the window, more in his head than seeing what was outside it. "Yeah, I'm fine, just taking in the sights."

"Well, take in this sight, everyone. We're here!"

Miguel looked up to see a large wooden sign with faded lettering that appeared older than Grandpa Emory: *Welcome to Green Hollow, the Shining Emerald of Massachusetts. Population: 600.* Bright yellow, burnt red, and brown leaves piled around the sign, threatening to engulf it. Wisps of wind blew fallen leaves in front of the car, and Miguel imagined the crunching sound they would make beneath the tires. Emma groaned as she stirred awake to the sound of Gideon's music blaring from the headphones he had just pulled out.

"Truck!" Wyatt yelled, "Truck. Truck!"

An old-looking truck was up ahead, pulled off to the left side of the road. Calling it blue would be a disservice to the tireless job the rust did covering the vehicle in its reddish-brown hues. The front driver's door was ajar, and its right rear light was busted and had probably been so for a long time. Just in front of it sat a police car with its lights off. As they drove by the vehicles, they appeared to be empty. That was enough for both Miguel and Benji to return to what they were doing. However, something about the scene piqued Emma's interest, and Miguel could see the gears of her imagination were already spinning. She sat up, alert, her eyes darted wildly as she leaned over Wyatt's car seat to press her forehead to the window.

"It. Was. Aliens!" She said in a matter-of-fact tone, "Aliens came and took them and did experiments on them!"

"Or they just ran out of gas," Gideon said.

"NO! It was aliens; I've seen videos about them."

"Truuuuck!" Wyatt whined as they passed by. Miguel wondered if Wyatt's speech was a bit behind for his age. He generally spoke in one-word sentences, if at all. He was more likely to grunt and point to what he wanted. He remembered noticing that when he first met the kids. That day had forever changed his life. He had been at a restaurant opening, preparing notes for an article that would tear their bland Malva pudding apart, when he got a phone call from Benji that made him drop his notepad and rush out of the restaurant to meet him.

The memory of Benji standing in front of the hospital with Gideon as he drove up would stick with him forever. He had never met Benji's family before that day and would never meet his brother and sister-in-law. He remembered how his stomach sank seeing Gideon. He had never seen someone look so broken. He couldn't help wondering if Wyatt's speech issues stemmed from what happened that day. The only thing that broke him out of his thoughts was the realization that they were driving through town. But the relief he felt was short-lived.

"It's amazing to think how much history my family has in this town, yet I have never set foot here once," said Benji. Miguel had a hard time paying attention to what his husband was saying due to the sheer panic he felt at noticing that none of the buildings were taller than two stories. There were several shops on either side. Cobblestone paths paved the narrow alleyways between structures. Pumpkins, scarecrows, and haystacks revealed an excitement for the changing seasons. Everything seemed to have been built long ago, except one building that did its best to appear old: a brewery with the town's name etched on the side of its all-wood structure. It seemed one of the busiest places, with a wooden deck on its side filled with people drinking and eating on barrel tables and log benches. At the center of the town was a statue of a large old boot with a plaque Miguel was unable to read from the van.

"That's it?" he said, realizing they had already reached the end of the town.

"I think it is quaint," Benji replied. Gideon let out a groan in solidarity with Miguel's frustration.

The winding road leading up to the Manor, tricky to traverse in their fully loaded Mini Van, had all but been reclaimed by nature and time. A bridge made it possible to drive over a river that went through the road. Once across it, thick stone walls shaped like two towers on either side with a stone arch covered with moss stood looming over a porch that wrapped around the front. Fallen leaves had settled across it like a thick blanket. There was a large garden off to the left; if he squinted hard, he could make out the shapes of several statues. The roof had a faded black look from years of harsh weather. Miguel started worrying about the number of repairs the old building would need. When he was a kid, he dreamed of living in a stone castle like a prince, but now that he had his palace, it felt more like he would be its groundskeeper than royalty.

"Looks like we're here," Benji said.

"Cooool," Emma whispered. Her eyes widened as if looking at her own royal palace. Miguel thought about how Emma must see the manor as he would have as a child. Able to see all the possibilities and get lost in creating the stories that this place could have. But for him, it was isolated, far from what he had been working toward. His entire life would be uprooted and locked away in one of these old stone towers. He knew he could not express the pain he felt staring at what would become his life. But he was amazed at how, despite the loss of her parents, Emma could still see so much hope in such a decrepit place. Perhaps he could make this work after all. *Click.*

Chapter 2

Two enormous wooden doors stood in front of Gideon. He took in the large Manor, which his father had only briefly mentioned. Whenever it did come up, it always had an unreal presence about it. Almost as if it existed in a different plane of reality from the lives he and his family lived. Yet, standing before the enormous building, memories began to flood back, memories of when his grandpa was still in his right mind and had told him stories about the place. He had never liked the air of mystery surrounding his family about the manor. The town existed thanks to his great, great, great, great, grandfather, or was it his great, great, great, grandfather? He couldn't remember. What he could remember is that the house and town held a prominent place in his family lineage, though no one had been back there for generations. Being the first Kavanagh to stand, there felt a lot like being the first person to walk on the moon since Neil Armstrong.

"Woah, woah, woah, no need to drag it!" Benji walked briskly to lift Emma's suitcase for her, "It doesn't have wheels; you have to carry it, see?"

"Can you carry it? I'm tired." Emma whined.

"Sure." As Benji picked up the bag, Emma darted, with renewed energy, around the corner. Gideon grinned and slowly shook his head, knowing how Emma was working him over. She could easily con an adult into doing just about anything for her. He liked Benji so far. He only had vague memories of him as a young kid, that was, up until a couple of months ago. And Miguel seemed like an alright guy. Gideon learned he was Dominican and a well-known New York food critic. He was a short man, Gideon guessed about 5' 5," on the leaner side with a five o'clock shadow and short, styled black hair.

"Benji, help me with your dad; I don't think he plans to get up and walk on his own anytime soon!" Miguel shouted from the car.

"I wasn't going to forget my own father!" Benji replied, taking his first step onto the wooden planks leading to the porch. The weight of his foot caused the already weakened step to give way. Gideon leaped forward and grabbed his uncle's arm before he could fall on his face. As Benji regained his balance, he lifted his foot from the broken step and looked sideways at Gideon.

"This bodes well."

"Could be worse, right?" Gideon said with a grin. The rest of the steps bore his and Benji's weight fine, and they were able to reach the doors with ease.

"I'll have to fix that later," Benji said. Gideon grabbed the door and pushed it open. He was shocked to notice it was already unlocked. The room smelled like an old bookstore he visited once during a school trip. An old lady ran it, and he remembered piles of old and forgotten books where a mean orange cat had made its bed. But unlike the cramped bookstore, the room he stood in was bare except for the carpet of dust that lay across everything. Dust floated in the air, exposed by the light from the window above the doors. A staircase on the left side of the room curved as it ascended to the second floor. From what Gideon could tell, the dark wood railing still seemed in good condition, and the steps were long and thick. He turned and saw his reflection looking back at him from an antique mirror on the adjacent wall.

He used to feel pride when people said he looked like his father. Now, he just felt guilt. Guilt for not going with them that night. A choice he felt he would live with forever. *Why didn't I just go to that stupid play?*

Instead, he stood in a creepy old house with his uncle, whom he hardly knew, and Miguel, who was sometimes hard work. His stomach sank, and for a moment, he feared he was slipping back into that dark place. Tears formed behind his eyes, and he cleared his throat. He felt a hand grip his shoulder as he almost rammed his head into the mirror. Turning around, his eyes met those of a young woman, and he felt a burst of heat flood his cheeks. She had a large, friendly smile and long, wavy brown hair.

"Sorry, I didn't mean to scare you," she said

He mustered his deepest voice and said, "It's fine."

"I called out to you, but I guess you couldn't hear. I'm Mary, the nurse to care for Emory." She held out her hand to Gideon.

He accepted her hand, giving it a light shake, "Oh, okay. So, you're the reason the door was unlocked."

"Yes, your father called and asked that I come ahead to set everything up." The doors swung open, revealing Benji carrying Emory into the house with Wyatt tugging at his leg, followed by Miguel lugging suitcases.

"Oh, please, let me help you!" Mary quickly walked over to help carry Emory into the adjacent study, where her medical equipment was set up. Benji exhaled, rubbing the back of his hand across his forehead as he put Emory down.

"Thank you, Mary." He turned around with a huge grin, "Gideon, go ahead and pick out your room."

"Perks of being the oldest, eh?" Mary added. Gideon made his way up to the second floor with his bags without looking back. He wondered if he could find a room that wasn't filled with cobwebs and dust. Unlikely. When he arrived at the last step, he noticed that to the left was a double doorway that he figured led to the master bedroom. He quickly turned his attention to the right, where other doors stood on either side, promising the possibility of more bedrooms.

He quickly assessed that the bedrooms were about the same size for the most part, except that the one furthest down the hall seemed to have the fastest access to the bathroom he would have to share. He made it to the bedroom and put his bags on the floor. The room was bare except for the cobwebs in the corner. He opened his luggage and retrieved a small picture in a black frame. He chuckled and rubbed his thumb across the surface to wipe away a smudge on his dad's face. It was just after the day he won his first match in his high school hockey team. "Gideon, you're going to go pro," his dad had said.

"Maybe, but you'll never see it now," he whispered, then shook his head, attempting to push the memory back down. He sat the picture down gingerly and then lay his back on the hardwood floor, staring at his new, somehow dusty, ceiling. Gideon was deep in thought, planning how to position his furniture and other things that were supposed to arrive next week, until he was jarred from his thoughts, realizing how clearly he could hear the others walking up the stairs.

" My room."

"No, Wyatt, This will mine Uncle Benji's room. There is a lovely room over…."

"My room."

"As I said, this is our room; let me take you to yours and…."

"MYYYYY ROOOOM!"

"Wyatt, no! Come back! Get off of that!"

Gideon smirked. He honestly believed his Uncle and Miguel were good people. Nothing about them really bothered him. But they didn't stand a chance.

Chapter 3

"Gotcha!" Emma said as she leaped to capture a small cricket that was too quick. Her elbows dug an inch into the ground, staining her white cardigan. "Shit!" she said, hoping no one heard. When she looked up, her eyes were drawn to a thick wall of trees that fenced in the area surrounding the mansion. Having a hard time looking away, she squinted deeper into the forest, which was so dense she could only see pitch black. She tried to look further, pushing herself up while brushing the dirt off her legs. She never looked away. Standing still, she felt as though the trees were moving closer, and she could hear the faint sound of a horn in the distance. Emma couldn't remember seeing any roads nearby besides the small one they had taken through town. It almost reminded her of city traffic, like she used to hear at home.

Another honk blasted out from the trees as if the road was getting closer. Frozen, her heart beat faster. The trees loomed even closer; the horn grew louder. Her surroundings became darker and darker until she felt smothered. Tires screeched. She collapsed into herself, cradling her head into her knees. For a moment, she saw her mother's face smiling back at her, one of those smiles that caused lines to appear near her eyes. Then, a blinding light engulfed her vision, and she felt the painful pressure of a seatbelt against her chest. The smell of smoke and metal filled the air. She remembered specks of glass in her mother's hair, drops of blood from her mother's lips, and the open but empty eyes that stared past her.

"Emma!" Miguel called out. She raised her head over her knees, her heart still racing, but as she looked around, everything appeared to be as before. These episodes had happened before. Not like that one, though. Not ever like that.

"Emma!" Miguel's voice reverberated around the side of the manor. She ran over to her uncle, trying her best to seem okay and hoping he would believe her sweat was from chasing crickets.

"Look at you! You've ruined another outfit running around like that. You know I have half a mind to buy you all brown clothes." He put his hands on his hips and smirked. "How about we just put you in brown paper bags, huh?" She rushed past him without bothering to respond. She would never let him know, but Miguel was not half bad in her mind, though maybe he was trying to kill her with his fancy dinners. After what had happened, she found sleeping nearly impossible most nights. So she gained a new appreciation for the sounds of dogs barking, cars driving past, and people speaking near the tiny apartment her uncles shared. One night, she had overheard them talk about whether or not they should keep Emma and her siblings. She knew it was an argument because her mom and dad sometimes had them, but Miguel had said, "This is a big decision, Benji! You are asking to completely change our lives here. Isn't there anyone else that can take them?"

"There isn't anyone! Only my dad who is incapable of taking care of himself."

"They don't even know you; you're like a stranger to them, como soy yo."

"What else can I do? They will grow up in the system if I don't take them. They need us."

"How on earth are you planning to afford this? We can't all just live in this one-bedroom apartment."

"Well, I actually have some ideas about that." Emma thought about that night often, which didn't make liking Miguel very easy. However, he had kept them, so that was something.

That night in their new home was the first time she had sat at a table for dinner in a long time. Thankfully, a few pieces of furniture had been left. The dining room was not very large compared to other rooms in the house, so the table sitting at least a dozen people fitted in tightly. Benji was incredibly excited about the table and serving pizza from the local pizzeria as if it were a ten-course meal. She didn't understand why the table was such a big deal or why adults always got excited about weird things like that. She remembered Benji saying that the wood was *buhogany* and a million years old, even older than Grandpa. She didn't think much about it except that it was hard to reach the top, and she would most likely need to sit on a pillow next time. She watched as Uncle Benji pushed Grandpa Emory over to the end of the table. He would not be able to eat much, but Uncle Benji wanted to make him feel included. That must be what doctors do, she thought to herself.

"I was looking through the basement and found a lot of the other furniture down there. Maybe tomorrow we can bring it up," said Miguel

"That sounds great," Benji replied

"Shouldn't be here," Emory uttered.

"We want to eat with you, Dad," said Benji

"Shouldn't be here. Not right." Emory replied with the same emotionless expression he always wore. Everyone chalked it up to his condition. Emma used to be afraid of Grandpa until Uncle Benji explained that he had something called *all-timers*. She asked if she would ever get all-timers, but Benji said it was unlikely.

"So yeah, tomorrow morning, you and Gideon can help me lift all that old stuff."

"Yeah, sure," said Gideon.

"Definitely not tonight," Miguel added.

"Why not? You scared?" Emma chided

"Uhh, definitely! How about you spend the night down there, missy!"

"Uh, no, that's dangerous!" she replied.

"Sounds like you're scared, too!"

THUMP. The sound came from upstairs, chilling the room. For a moment, everyone stared at each other wide-eyed. Then, after a few more moments, the grownups exhaled heavily.

"Well, old house, odd sounds," Benji said to break the silence.

Gideon bent over toward Wyatt and whispered loud enough for everyone to hear, "Maybe it's a ghost." Wyatt shrieked, clutching his brother's arm playfully. They laughed until another thump came from above.

Chapter 4

———————

Sunlight poured through the tall, narrow window, warming half of Gideon's face. He reached for his phone to check the time, only to groan; they still had no bars. He assumed that hillbillies up in the mountains had at least one bar, but not here in the deep forests of Massachusetts. He had figured that contact with his friends in New York would dwindle; now, he guessed it would halt entirely.

Gideon quickly threw some clothes on and went to Emma's room. He felt responsible for his sibling these days. The last thing Gideon needed was for them to misbehave so much that his uncles decided it was too complicated and put them into state care. He knocked lightly and opened Emma's door to find it empty, so he rushed to Wyatt's to find it was also empty. They must be awake already, he thought. He checked his phone a second time; it read 8:05. As he turned the corner, Gideon noticed his uncle's door open just enough to see the outlines of two men with one small boy sprawled between them. Wyatt must have come back last night and reclaimed the master bedroom. He stood there amused, unable to help a light chuckle at Wyatt's hand lying across Miguel's face.

His attention quickly focused on a sound downstairs. It was a mixture of crashing dishes and hurried footsteps. He rushed downstairs to see what the commotion was. When he arrived in the kitchen, he saw Emma trying desperately to clean up the mess from a broken bowl and cereal spread across the floor. When she noticed Gideon standing there, she jumped in surprise.

"I'm cleaning it up. I was hungry. I swear, I'm doing it right now. You don't need to tell anyone. You don't want me to starve, so let me clean this, okay?" Emma said, fumbling her words.

"Mhm," Gideon replied, a little annoyed. He settled for helping her clean up the mess. Not long after he had knelt to pick up pieces, a half-awake Miguel appeared in the doorway.

"What's going on?"

"Just cleaning up a small mess," Gideon replied

"A mess? Well, I guess I must take all of your stuff!" He paused momentarily and brought his hand to his chin to stroke his beard before asking, "Where is your stuff again?" Gideon and Emma looked at each other.

"The moving van," she answered.

"Ah! So, when your stuff arrives, we will unpack it, put it away, and forbid you to touch it as a punishment. How does that sound?" Miguel said.

"No way! Emma yelled.

Gideon couldn't help but burst into laughter, "It's just a joke."

"Here, let me help," Miguel said as he leaned down to pick up the shattered bowl. "So Benji plans to get some stuff set up for his work. Gideon, do you mind coming into town with me and Wyatt to run some errands?"

Gideon wasn't sure about spending a whole day with Miguel, but the idea of exploring the town piqued his interest, "Yeah, that sounds good."

They parked beside the town strip, where the only paved road was freshly finished. Gideon sensed that Miguel didn't want to be seen driving a minivan. Most of the shops lined this area surrounding the center. There stood that old giant boot he saw when they first drove through town. Nothing was happening; a few people walked the cobblestone strip, passing the shops.

Wyatt grabbed Gideon's hand and tugged. "See that?"

"What?"

"That!" Wyatt pointed

"The big boot?" he asked.

"Big boot! Big boot!" Wyatt said, pulling Gideon toward it.

Gideon looked at Miguel, who patted his pocket, checking for his wallet, and let his brother lead him over to the statue.

"I'll let you guys check things out while I go to those shops."

Gideon took Wyatt to the square where the giant boot stood. Wyatt looked up at the statue with wide eyes and a huge smile that, for some reason, faded into a frown. He watched his little brother sizing up his own foot and quickly realized he was disheartened with his leg brace.

"Hey, you know when that brace comes off, I'm going to buy you a bigger boot than this one? We can even live in it if you want." He ruffled his Wyatt's hair and received a smile.

Gideon knelt beside the placard just on the front of the statue, which read:

The giant's boot, it does now sit
who created this town without any wit
If ever a man, this boot would fit
Giant's blood, he must admit.

Gideon stood up and scratched his head momentarily, "Can you make any sense of that?"

Wyatt shook his head as they stood there staring at the enormous boot.

"It describes the town legend," a new voice said from behind. Gideon turned to see a young girl around his age with long brown hair and hazel eyes partially covered by thick purple glasses. She was much shorter than him, almost as short as Miguel. She had several necklaces, each with a different colored stone at the end of it. Her fingers fiddled with one that was brown and gold.

"The legend is about how this town was created. It involves a giant stepping into the middle of this forest," she gestured around them with her free hand, "He helped make this little town of ours."

"So I'm guessing you're the town historian," Gideon said, smiling.

"Just someone who has lived here her entire life; everyone here knows the story." She smiled, releasing the necklace and letting it rest beside the others.

"My name is Gideon, and this is my little brother, Wyatt."

"Hi Wyatt, cool brace."

Wyatt hid his face behind Gideon's leg.

She looked at Gideon, "So, I assume you guys are new here."

"You assume right! Just moved here yesterday, actually, from New York."

She approached the boot, letting her hand graze the placard. "That's a pretty big city to move from."

"Have you ever been?" Gideon asked.

She turned back to him, smiling sheepishly. "No, I've lived here since birth."

"You definitely should try and visit. There's so much more to do there than in this little town."

Her smile faded. "Little town, huh? This little town may not have all the amenities you're used to, but we have some good people here willing to help each other out."

Gideon furrowed his brow, "Hey now, I didn't mean anything by that."

"Oh, I'm sure." She looked him up and down, "I'm guessing you're an Aries, then?"

"Well, uh yeah, actually." After a few awkward moments of silence, Gideon was shaken out of it by Wyatt gripping his leg, "Alright, Wyatt, how about we find Uncle Miguel now. I think I've had enough of the sights," he said, brushing past her.

He tried to make a swift exit, but Wyatt's brace slowed them down, making for an awkward escape. They arrived at the shop, and Gideon could hear Miguel from outside. He paused to look at Wyatt, taking in a deep breath before entering.

"Gideon! Look at all the great stuff they have here! I was able to find all kinds of good produce, and look, I even found Emma this lovely little doll."

Gideon raised an eyebrow at the odd way his uncle was acting; his smile was all teeth, and his eyes seemed too large. He reached into his Basket and pulled out an old-fashioned porcelain doll that had a pull string on the back, which he pulled on, causing it to say,

"Hi, my name is Emma! Can we be friends?"

"Wow, that doll is creepy..." Gideon was interrupted by Miguel clearing his throat and gesturing with his eyes to his left. Gideon followed his gaze to a plump, smiley woman staring them both down. He realized instantly what Miguel was doing.

"That doll is so cool. Really cool. I'm sure Emma's going to love it!" he said, putting on a faker smile than a beauty pageant contestant.

They finished at the store. Gideon noticed that Miguel bought a bunch of roots, extracts, and other things he hadn't ever seen before. On the way out, Miguel looked over his shoulder at him and mumbled, "The selection here is awful. They wouldn't know the difference between turmeric and ginger root if I hit them over the head with it." Gideon shook his head. They checked out a few more shops before heading home. As they walked, Gideon noticed two old men arguing, one on a ladder and the other holding it for support.

"Ol' Henry was a drunk, Roy! You know he was bound to get himself either thrown out of town or into a cell."

"He never bothered me none."

"That's because your too thick to be bothered; hold that ladder steady!"

"Why did he leave his truck behind, then? He loved that thing more than all three of his ex-wives combined."

"That old rusty thing was bound to have him peddling it with his feet once that floor fell out. Steady Roy!" He snapped as the ladder wobbled beneath him, "Keep this thing still, or I'm going to volunteer you for the pie-throwing booth!"

"I'm not even showing up for that silly fall festival, Carl!" Roy replied

"Oh, you'll show up like the rest of us; not like you got anything better going on."

The two grumbled on, their voices fading away as Gideon made it to the van. He opened the side door and lifted his brother into his seat, "Did you hear those guys, Wyatt? I guess there's going to be some kind of festival soon. Sounds pretty cool, huh?"

"Cool!" Wyatt said.

Once home, Gideon helped put away groceries while his uncle told him stories about his college days, "I started as a psychology major, which, you know, is just an attempt to get free therapy. Then I went into the English department; I really thought I was the next Poe. All dark and dreary, it turned out I was just dramatic. So, then I tried theatre, but I kept forgetting my lines, so that was a pass. Finally, I made my way into the culinary arts department, and it stuck."

Gideon stared at the large green, spiky-looking melon on the counter that Miguel had picked out, "What is that ugly thing?" Miguel followed his gaze.

"Oh, that? It's called a Jack fruit! Super good for you. Tastes great with barbeque." Gideon forced a smile and nodded politely.

Emma poked her head around the corner. What's all the noise about?" He saw her staring at the jack fruit on the counter, "Why is there an alien egg in the kitchen?"

"It's a Jack fruit," Gideon replied

Emma scrunched up her face, "Fruit. Sure."

"Oh hey, I picked this up for you while I was out." Miguel took out the Doll to give it to her, "It's hand-crafted."

"Oh. This is, well, this is so great," she said, receiving the creepy doll, "Thanks, Miguel. I can't wait to put it in my room," probably meaning in a locked box in her room's closet.

"Pull the string!" Gideon coaxed

When she did, her eyes filled with terror, and she was only able to repeat the words, "Well, this is so great."

Chapter 5

As the rest of the family went on with their day, trying to get comfortable in their new surroundings, Wyatt explored the nooks and crannies that others would miss or overlook. He had already found plenty of hidden areas around the house like spaces under the staircase and little rooms possibly used for storage. He walked into the room where they kept Grandpa and noticed he was muttering to himself. Saying things like, "She's listening, always listening." And, "Why did we come here? We weren't supposed to."

Mary entered the room with a tray of food, "Look what I got for you, Emory; Miguel made it." She paused, looking down at the bowl before adding, "He called it chicken with cream sauce and green chili mash, and well, it looks like fancy tomato soup with a piece of chicken on top to me. Oh, Wyatt! I didn't see you there, kiddo; thanks for watching your grandpa for me. Why don't you go and play."

Wyatt didn't need any convincing since he was afraid of Grandpa. So, he left the room to explore upstairs, leaving behind his family, who were more focused on their tasks than watching him. He had trouble getting up the stairs, but not as much as everyone thought. His brace clanked on each step, but he pushed himself up with both hands until he made his way to the second floor.

Wandering upstairs, he did his best impression of a superhero, flying by each room as he made his way down the dark hallway. He passed by doors as he made swoosh noises with his mouth. The superhero name Emma gave him back in their old home was Metal Man due to his brace. He imagined that despite the clanking sound it made, he was capable of flying anywhere he wanted. He was brave as he ventured deeper into the unlit hallway. *Creeeeeeeek.*

Wyatt turned to look back and saw a door had opened. He was brave, so he went to investigate. As he stood in the frame of the new room, the darkness within appeared to go on forever. Despite how hard he tried, Wyatt could not see anything inside. He was scared of it, but a superhero did not fear the dark, so he entered the room to look for a light. As he stepped forward, the only sound that could be heard was the clanking of his brace. It was as if the darkness engulfed him, making the hair on his arms stand up. He started pressing on the walls to find a light switch. Eventually, he felt one and hopped to flick it to the on position. Gideon would have been upset if he had seen him jumping in his brace. The light flickered on with a hum and helped to illuminate the small room.

In the center was an old-looking box with chipped paint and symbols Wyatt did not understand. He walked over to it and, without hesitation, opened the lid that lifted on old metal hinges. For Wyatt, what was inside could only be described as an utter disappointment. A bunch of old photos with people he didn't know. He thought maybe he could use the box for toys, so he picked it up and carried it to his room. It took him a lot of effort to move, and he had to use the wall to support him at times, but eventually, he made it to his room and poured the photos into his closet. For a moment, he stared at one picture in particular. It was of a man wearing a suit and a big hat and a pretty lady wearing a white dress. There was something about the picture that he liked, so he took it and put it back in the box.

Chapter 6

"Miguel is trying to kill me!" Emma declared in the backseat of the car.

"Kill you? How so?" Benji replied, looking at her through the rearview mirror.

"He wants me to be made fun of! Look at everything he has me wearing!" She waved her hands franticly, pointing out her outfit. It was a bright yellow dress with an olive-green jacket and an ivory scarf that matched her small heels. She didn't even know what ivory meant. "Why can't I wear my jeans and T-shirts!"

Benji shook his head. "Uncle Miguel just got a little excited, is all. I'm sure he will calm down once we get used to things."

"I stick out like a sore thumb!"

"He just wants you to be comfortable."

"He just wants me to be laughed out of school." She said as she pouted, looking out the window.

"I think you look very pretty." Emma could not help but blush, which made her all the angrier.

"I just want to blend in." The car pulled into the school parking lot, crowded with other vehicles and kids getting out of them. She felt a tinge of panic, and her stomach swirled uncomfortably as she inched closer to being dropped off. "Maybe I can be homeschooled?"

"Unless you want to be lectured all day on the differences between mincing and chopping food, I don't think you want Miguel teaching you."

"Good point." She agreed. She took in a deep breath and prepared herself, "Hey, are those teenagers?"

"No, they are middle schoolers. This school is combined," Benji replied.

"This really is a small town."

Benji stopped and turned to Emma, "Now I want you to storm this new school like the beaches of Normandy! Have a great day, kid." Emma shook her head and exited the van, thinking that she didn't know what Normandy was, but she would have much preferred it to what was to come.

The school was much like her old one: brick walls, crowded halls, and a lunchroom filled with odd smells. Some kids rushed to class, and others gathered in groups blocking hallways. It didn't take her long to read the map and find homeroom. She walked in feeling a bit more confident that she would still be able to blend in, given the kids she saw. She opened the door and quickly changed her mind. The room that was previously filled with laughter fell as silent as a kid who had just broken something expensive. Every kid was staring at her, some even sizing her up. One girl in particular with curly blonde hair and braces marched right up to her. "Hi, I'm Cindy. My mother is head of the PTA here," she said. Emma faked a smile.

"Hi, my name's Emma."

Cindy looked her up and down. "Are you color blind, Emma?"

"No?"

"Well, wherever you're from, you must lack the ability to see color. Because you don't match." The class laughed, all except one boy in the back. She didn't get a chance to respond because the teacher, Mr. Backer, motioned for her to come over. She walked to his desk in front of a large blackboard. He was a tall, lanky man with a balding head and gray hair.

"It's nice to meet you, Emma. You'll be sitting over there at the desk in the front." Emma didn't reply but nodded and walked to her seat, feeling heat creep into her cheeks. She absolutely hated this school and, at that moment, Miguel.

After a grueling hour or two, the bell rang, indicating the end of the first period and the beginning of recess. Emma decided to wait until the other kids had already left before getting up and heading to the playground. As she moved to leave, Mr. Baker stopped her, "Hey, Emma. I found this pair of sneakers in the lost and found if you want to try them; I'm sure heels will make playing difficult." She turned to see a pair of white beat-up sneakers in Mr. Baker's hand and smiled.

Emma walked onto the playground, noticing groups of kids playing different games. A small group of girls, including Cindy, giggled while whispering back and forth. Some boys near a seesaw were attempting to catapult rocks over the high fence. She smiled, thinking about joining the boys, when she noticed the kid from class who hadn't laughed at her, nose-deep in a book. She started over to him when a rock smacked into one of the metal trash cans on the other side of the fence and brought the attention of the teacher, who quickly ran over to chase the offending kids away. Emma's gaze was then drawn to a nearby roundabout that was spinning on its own. It made a screeching noise, she guessed, due to the old nature of the equipment. The screeching sounded louder and louder the more Emma focused on it. Screeching like the tires of a car. Screeching before the car. *BANG!*

The sound of Cindy's confetti popper made Emma fall backward, scraping the back of her heel. The other girls in her group began to laugh and jump around her. Emma felt as if her heart was beating a million miles a second. She could barely breathe, and her eyes went wild. She couldn't focus on one single child that was skipping around her.

"Oh, Come on, Emma; you can't be THAT much of a baby," Cindy jibed. Cindy's words sent Emma into a rage that was animal-like in nature, instantly putting the other girls on edge. She stood up, dusting herself off, and then, without a moment of hesitation, leaped at Cindy, knocking her to the ground. Thrashing at her with her hands, Cindy was only able to get a few good hits in with her palm. None of the girls went to help their friend, who was screaming at the top of her lungs. "You're crazy! Get off, you psycho!" she yelled.

The teacher who was chasing the boys finally noticed and pulled at Emma, who was still thrashing and growling. Emma looked around and saw how the other children's eyes were wide with horror; no one was laughing now. She looked to her left to see the boy who had been reading earlier, gripping the book for dear life and nervously watching from the doorway. As Emma was being escorted back inside, she turned to the boy and smiled a big bloody grin.

Chapter 7

Miguel was hard at work. He pulled most of the furniture that was salvageable out of the basement and started to fix up each room. Wyatt played in the adjacent room. Miguel began in the front parlor, where he placed several comfortable but worn chairs in front of the fireplace and put a small table between them. Placing his baby blue coffee cup on the small table, he wiped down the chairs and sanitized them the best he could. Some of the restaurants Miguel had been to would have paid an insane amount of money to replicate this aesthetic. He took a sip of his coffee and placed it on the table, then began to vacuum around the chairs.

He remembered the time he went to a tasting where the food was eaten in the dark. It was supposed to accentuate the senses to bring out the flavors. He later wrote in his review that it only helped to bring out the blandness of the shrimp scampi. Miguel chuckled to himself, unsure if anyone else would have found it so humorous. He then took another sip of his coffee and noticed a large portrait of a grey stone lighthouse sitting on a cliff. It was crooked. He brought his coffee over to the mantle. Adjusting the picture, he took a step back to check his work. Approving the correction, he reached over to pick up his mug but grasped at thin air. Looking down, he noticed it was missing from the mantle place. Worried that it had fallen, he looked at the floor around him, but there was no sign of a mess. He looked around to see where his favorite cup could have gone, but it had vanished. He stood for a moment, his mind searching for a possible reason for his coffee mug to have disappeared. He looked around for Wyatt but saw him still in the adjacent room, playing with his dinosaurs. He realized there was no way Wyatt could have reached the mantle by himself, especially with his leg brace, so he decided to believe that he must have never brought the coffee cup to the mantle at all. But where was it?

Knock, knock. Miguel jumped at the sound. It came again, and he headed for the door with no idea who would be stopping by. He swung the door open, clearing his throat, and was met by a woman who appeared to be about his age. She had bleach-blonde hair, the kind that had been dyed so many times the ends were stiff and frayed. It came to the middle of her thick neck, which, just like her round face, was caked in makeup. She raised a casserole dish, pressing it toward Miguel. He had little choice but to take it.

"Hey! My name is Brandy-Sue, and I'm your new neighbor."

Miguel leaned forward, poking his head out, and looked around; he was sure there were no other houses for miles. "Hi…"

"I see y'all are settling in just fine. I was just telling my husband how amazing it is that someone moved into this house. He said no one would ever want to move into this creepy old place, but here y'all are."

Miguel raised an eyebrow. "Brandy?"

"Brandy-Sue! My husband is the town orthodontist, I'm the homemaker, except I rarely spend any time at home." She laughed. "What does your husband do?"

Miguel's eyes widened. "Benji is starting a practice here." He was half surprised he could get more than two words out.

"Oh, he is the one replacing Doctor Hatch! Doctor Hatch is a sweet old man with gentle hands. Look at us, both married to doctors."

"Yes, well, thank you for the Casserole…"

"Do you mind if I come in and look around?" Brandy-Sue interrupted.

"Um." Miguel took a moment to look over his shoulder and see Wyatt playing in the other room, "We aren't really unpacked yet…"

"That's totally fine with me; I can help you out!" She pushed by him. "I am a homemaker, after all." She did a complete turn scanning the house, "Huh, why have you got a broom nailed up there?"

"It's a family tradition. Something my Grandma did."

"Well, that is just so special!" Miguel looked down at the disaster of a green bean casserole. He sighed and closed the door behind him. He knew he would eventually have to get acquainted with the town; he just didn't expect the town to come to his front porch. "Wow, wow, wow, WOW!" Brandy-sue let out as she looked around, "This place is huge!" The only thing more annoying than hearing her voice was hearing it echo back at him. He couldn't wait to finish filling out the rooms.

"Yeah, It is a lot bigger than the apartment we moved from."

"New York, right? The Big Apple? You two don't strike me as small-town types."

"Well, yes, you are correct."

"That's so great! My husband and I have lived here almost our whole lives!" Brandy-Sue looked over to see Wyatt playing with his dinosaurs in the other room, "You have a child!" Wyatt lowered his dinosaur and stared at her inquisitively.

"That's Wyatt. Come over here, buddy; come say hi." Wyatt shook his head, got up, and started limping away.

"Poor thing," said Cindy, loud enough for Wyatt to hear. Miguel watched as Wyatt stiffened. It was only for a moment, but he knew how self-conscious the boy was about his leg. Miguel frowned. "What happened to his leg?" she asked.

"His legs didn't grow straight. He needs the brace to help."

"Oh, bowlegged. Well, he still reminds me of my own sweet boy." Brandy-Sue was on the move again, exploring what she could of the bottom floor until she reached the kitchen with Miguel in tow. "Love the cabinet space."

"Thank you. Uh, it's one of my favorite rooms in the house," Miguel replied, thinking he wouldn't want to change the dark green wall or the hardwood floors. He set the casserole on the table in the center of the room. "Places like this are for homemakers like us, right? There was a hint of bitterness in his voice. Homemaker. Why did it feel so silly to use that word? That's what he was now. Yet somehow, it didn't feel right. It didn't feel like him.

"I actually don't cook much," said Cindy.

"Oh."

She leaned against the counter. "Yeah, I bought that and put it in a dish. Figure that's what a good neighbor is supposed to do." Miguel couldn't help but laugh. "So, how did you and your husband meet?" There was an eagerness in the way her eyes lit up. Miguel knew she was the type of person who loved being in the know.

"I was working, trying a restaurant's new peanut sorbet, when I had a bad reaction to it. I was rushed to the hospital, and Benji was the doctor on call that night. I won't lie; when I went home that night, I wrote that restaurant one of the best reviews it's ever had. Brandy-Sue squealed. Miguel remembered the way Benji had smiled at him and how easy it was to talk to him. The night after he had signed his discharge paperwork and was no longer a patient, Benji had come to him. Miguel was slipping on his jacket, just ready to head out, when Benji had stopped him at the door.

"There's this restaurant near my house," he said, shifting the paperwork he held between his hands. "They have this pizza; it's great. It has these green sour things on it."

"Banana peppers?"

"Yes, those. You should really give it a try… with me." Agreeing to that date was one of the best decisions Miguel had ever made. Rushed footfalls caught his ear, and he saw Mary turn the corner before noticing her in the kitchen. "Is everything alright?" Miguel was just about to introduce her to Brandy-Sue when Brandy came charging over.

"Mary! How are you? Haven't seen you around town in a few weeks." She leaned in for a hug. Mary accepted with a warm smile.

"I'm great. Just started my new job, which I'm sure you've heard all about." She grinned. Miguel was about to chime in when the phone rang. He was surprised to see any life come from his phone due to the poor coverage they had. When he looked down to check it, he saw that the caller ID said Green Hollow Elementary. He quickly accepted the call.

"Mr. Kavanagh?"

"Yes, This is Miguel Kavanagh."

"Right, I am sitting here with your daughter, Emma."

"Oh, Oooh." Miguel instantly realized what kind of call this was based on his own experiences as a child. "Is everything okay?"

"Well, not exactly, sir; Emma here got in a fight with another girl."

"Oh, my Lord!" Brandy-Sue said out loud, making it clear she had been eavesdropping.

"Listen, I can try and be down there soon, but my husband has the car."

"I can drive you! I have the Hummer outside!"

Miguel cringed and took a long moment before he said, "I'll be right there." The phone disconnected.

"I'm sick of the service in this old house always cutting out!" He looked at his phone and then remembered, "Wyatt! We need to round him up first."

"I can watch him while you're gone," Mary responded, "It's no trouble, really." Miguel agreed with the plan and turned to leave when his eyes were drawn to the kitchen table. He felt a cold shiver down his spine when he saw the baby blue coffee mug sitting there.

Chapter 8

"It seems we got disconnected," said Principal Connor. Emma sat in one of three chairs against the wall. He had already called Cindy's mom before Miguel, which didn't take as many tries but had left the 6-foot-tall man visibly shaken. He had been verbally abused by Cindy's mom for thirty minutes about allowing her child to be mauled by some rabid kid on his watch. Cindy's mother had threatened several lawsuits and ended the call with a dramatic statement of how the school system failed to protect her child. Now, Emma and Principal Connor sat quietly across each other.

"Listen, Emma, You seem like a good kid. However, you're making some not-so-good decisions." He sat up a little straighter in his chair and picked up a folder, "I read your file. I know you didn't move here in the best of circumstances. What you've been through, well, there are no words I can say to quantify that. However, if you need an ear, someone to talk to, my door is always open." Emma nodded but remained silent, turning her head to look out the door. She didn't believe anyone could really understand what she was going through. She didn't feel in control of her own head. Right then, all she really wanted was to not sit in silence while this adult stared at her with pity.

"Principal Connor, Miguel Kavanagh is in the front office," the administrative assistant poked her head in to say. Emma jumped out of her seat and rushed to the door.

"Emma, you can go back to your seat; your dad will come here."

Emma turned around and walked awkwardly to her seat, muttering to herself, "He's not my dad." A few moments passed, and then Miguel walked in, looking as anxious as Emma imagined she did. Principal Connor gestured for him to take a seat next to Emma, and Miguel complied as if he was being asked to point out a criminal in a police line-up.

He cleared his throat, "So, What happened?"

"Well, as I said before on the phone, Emma here got into a fight with one of the other girls in her class. It became rather violent with several scratch marks on the other girl as well as Emma taking a few good blows to the face." Miguel looked over at her. Fixated on the bruise forming on her chin. She looked away, embarrassed.

"Well, is the other girl in trouble?" Miguel asked.

"The other girl was the one who was assaulted," the principal replied.

"Yes, Emma may have hit her first, but what did she do to cause it?" Emma looked over at Miguel in surprise. She didn't expect him to defend her.

"All I am saying is Emma isn't a psychopath. If she chose to start swinging at some other kid, there was a reason for it."

"Mr. Kavanagh, there is no reason for violence."

"Oh, that is crap!"

Principal Connor raised an eyebrow, "Excuse me?"

"That is absolute crap! You mean to tell me, after all these years, that schools are still saying that!" He turned to Emma and said, "What did that little 'angel' do to you?"

"She popped a confetti popper in my face."

"A confetti popper in your face?"

"And then mocked me."

"And then mocked you?" Miguel did a double take. Looked at her and decided to go for it, "You know what, bullying takes many forms! We weren't there! I want to know why my Emma is sitting here taking all the blame while the other girl isn't."

"Because her mother has already picked her up," Principal Connor said dryly. "Listen, I appreciate your passion, but I still had to write an incident report. I won't suspend Emma this time, but I recommend she talk to the guidance counselor. She is free to go; that is why you are here." Miguel stood up self-righteously, taking Emma's hand and giving the principal one last glare before marching out of the office, pulling Emma along behind him. Just outside the door, where the principal couldn't hear, Miguel stopped to look her up and down,

"I don't know where you got those awful sneakers, but we are burning them when we get home." Emma nodded. Once outside, Emma could see a tank of a car sitting at the curb with a strange blonde woman waving at her. She became concerned when she realized Miguel was heading straight for the tank car. Next to the lady stood the little boy, whom Emma had smiled at before being dragged into the principal's office. The ride with the boy, who she learned was named Channing, was quick and awkward. His mother babbled on and on while Miguel sat next to her in silence. Occasionally, Emma looked over at Channing, wondering how destiny had brought them together. She decided that she would not stop until she made him her new best friend. Lucky him.

Emma was relieved to be home. The parents went straight inside. Miguel darted right for the door while Channing's mother continued her story. He didn't appear to pay any attention to her rambling. Emma watched as Channing sat down on the porch swing and opened his book. She raised an eyebrow and placed both hands on her hips. What was this boy's deal? He had a huge yard to play in, and he was sitting down to read? She sized him up for a moment and noticed again that he was very pale, almost like he never played outside. She decided this just wouldn't do. Emma walked over and plopped herself beside Channing.

"Watchya reading?"

He scooted further away from her. "Frankenstein."

"Cool, that's cool…. Wanna play?"

"Nah, I'm just waiting for my mom."

Emma saw through the window that Channing's mother was still blabbing on. "I'm sure you have plenty of time." She nudged his arm. "Come on." Channing sat his book down on the wooden swing and stared at her. Emma didn't wait for an answer; she grabbed his wrist and pulled him off the swing. They went around the side of the house where the thick forest met the backyard.

"Let's play…" she tapped a finger to her chin. "Hide and seek."

"Classic," Channing replied.

"You're the guest, so I'll count first." She was surprised to see an actual smile on the boy's face. Turning to face the wall of the house, she saw him dart away out of the corner of her eye.

"One… Two… Three…" Emma heard Channing shuffle past her as if he weren't picking his feet up as he walked. "You're going to have to hide further away than that." For a moment, it was silent, and so she continued, "Four… Five… Six…" Again, she heard Channing's feet shuffling a few feet away from her. He was near enough that she felt the wind brush off his body as he passed by. "Seriously, you have to hide further away. Have you ever even played this game before?"

36

Emma whipped around, fully expecting to see Channing standing not far behind her, but he wasn't there. The space was still and empty. She couldn't help but feel a sudden shiver. Either the kid was faster than a cheetah, or something else was out here. That did not deter Emma from her seeker responsibilities. She looked around and determined that the only good place to hide in this big open space would be in the woodline. Rushing over to the enormous trees, she stopped just before entering, realizing how much they towered over her. The trees were so thick that they created a canopy blocking her vision of the sky, except for the rays of light that spotted the ground. Despite how lovely the trees appeared, a looming fear entered her mind as she neared the first line. Suddenly, she felt a presence weighing on her, as if the gravity in this place was stronger. She approached the first tree she thought Channing might be hiding behind, jumping around it to catch him. When she discovered he wasn't there, she turned, scanning the nearby trees until her eyes became drawn to another one. It appeared to have something carved into it. As she approached, she admired the curved lines of the symbols. They seemed to knot into each other. She reached out her hand to trace the lines.

"Emma!" Channing shouted.

"You were supposed to be hiding," she said, shoving him.

Channing regained his balance, "I got scared; you took a while."

"What does this mean." She said, gesturing toward the carving.

He leaned in to inspect it. "Oh, this? Yeah, these things are everywhere in town."

"What do they mean?"

"I don't really know; people in town talk about them being here since the Irish immigrated here."

"What's immigrated?"

"It means they moved here."

Channing's mom called her son from the house, and they took off running in that direction. As Emma left the woods, she felt the heaviness of the forest lift.

Chapter 9

Fitting in was something Gideon excelled at. Convincing everyone around him that he was not some charity case to feel sorry for was what he set out to do from the start, making a good first impression. It was the last period of the day. Although the teacher did his very best to keep the attention of his class, Gideon held court in the back, telling stories of the Big Apple and his hockey successes.

"I played in front of this talent scout once, and the guy was really impressed with me. He said he'd be interested in maybe trying me out for a pro league in a couple of years." Gideon said. Everyone lapped up his stories. He even got a few approving nods from the teacher they were all ignoring. But one student made it clear she was uninterested. Agatha sat three rows away in the front, taking notes and, every once in a while, glancing back skeptically as if she didn't believe anything he said. Gideon did his best to seem unfazed by her apparent disregard for him. Still, he couldn't help but catch himself looking over at her to gauge if anything he was saying was making a dent in her thick armor.

"You got to try out!" someone behind him said. Gideon turned around and saw a chubby, dorky-looking kid with blonde pomade-styled hair and a big mouth with two large teeth in the front. "I'm sorry, what?"

"Fall tryouts, man! My hockey team is looking for fresh blood. I totally got the 'in' if you're interested." The guy didn't look like a hockey player type, but Gideon figured a small town like this just took whatever they could find.

"Oh yeah? I mean, I'll think about it. Have to get settled in first and all." He had no interest in returning to the ice, not without him. He couldn't help but notice that he had finally caught Agatha's attention. He smiled at her, and she returned the smile but with a little less certainty. *Ring, Ring.* The last bell sounded, saving Gideon from any further interactions, or at least he thought. He was on his way out the door when the chubby hockey player caught up with him.

"Hey, by the way, I'm Miles."

Gideon looked at him, continuing his stride. "Hey, Miles, nice to meet you. I've got to get to my uncle; he is probably waiting outside."

"Yeah, cool, totally cool, man. I'll catch up with you tomorrow!"

"Sure..." Gideon briskly made his way through the exit. When outside, he stood for a moment, looking around and seeing small groups of other students huddled together. They talked about their day, how stupid their teachers were, and how excited they were about fall break and the festival. Gideon's focus was drawn to a couple of faculty members who talked in hushed voices about the missing person.

"Can you believe they still haven't found Henry?" the first one said.

The other chimed in, "The poor guy left his truck behind. He loved that old, rusted thing."

"The Sheriff still thinks he might have just gone on another one of his drink benders."

"For almost a week?" The second shook his head, "I knew Henry liked his whiskey, but damn!"

"Yeah, maybe he just stumbled into the forest drunk and got lost."

"I guess Henry is out of the pie-eating competition this year."

"Yeah, that might give one of us a chance!"

Gideon thought how strangely morbid the townsfolk were. He was so focused on the two talking that he hadn't noticed his Uncle Benji waving at him from inside that awful minivan until it was too late. Gideon did his best to draw as little attention as possible. When he entered the van, he turned and saw Agatha standing on the front steps with a friend, talking. She was fiddling with one of the stones she wore around her neck. She looked directly at him, and Gideon shrunk in his seat. He turned his face so that she wouldn't see his embarrassment. Uncle Benji slowly drove away from the school. There was a long silence. Benji could see his uncle from the corner of his eye and start to speak before changing his mind. After what felt like an eternity, he decided to make the first move.

"So, how was work?" Gideon asked.

"Oh, fine, fine. Things are much quieter around here, so there's not much to do. How was school?"

"It was school."

"Good, good..."

There was something about the way he said it that caught Gideon off guard. For just a second, he could have sworn it was his father speaking. His chest tightened, and his mind went back to a memory of his dad cleaning the dirt off his pants and wiping his hands. He smelled of old books. His father had just pulled another box from the attic when Gideon noticed a stack of old photos in the box he was carrying. He was about six years old and loved helping his father around the house. "Who are these kids, Daddy?" he had asked, holding up a photo of two boys building a sandcastle on the beach. His father had leaned down, squinting his eyes.

"Ah, that's your Uncle Benji and I when we were little." He smiled, but there was a hint of sadness behind it that even the six-year-old Gideon had noticed. It wasn't until he was much older that he realized why his father always appeared sad when talking about his brother. He overheard his mother and father talking about his uncle's wedding invitation.

"I can't go, Emily; you know how my dad is."

"It just doesn't seem right." His mom reached out her hand to touch his dad's shoulder, "Benji's your brother, Jacob."

His dad took her hand in his and raised it to his lips, "You know my dad would cut us off if we went. He has done so much for us."

"Okay, whatever you feel is right."

As the van turned into the old road leading to the manor, Gideon realized that he must have been daydreaming for some time. He looked over at his uncle, who focused his attention on the road and, for a moment, thought how strange life could be. He had never had any contact with his uncle before living in the old manor house with him.

Chapter 10

"Our kids get along so well! I've never seen Channing take to someone so quickly!" Brandi-Sue said. Miguel looked over at the two kids playing in the front parlor while Mary checked Grandpa Emory's vitals.

"Yeah, Emma seems to really enjoy his company." He turned to see Brandi-Sue's face beaming with the same excitement as a kettle about to whistle.

"You MUST come with us to the fall festival," she said, clapping her hands enthusiastically. "It happens every year."

The front doors opened, and Benji and Gideon walked through. Miguel quickly made his way to them. "Here are my boys!" Miguel said, causing Gideon and Benji to exchange a look of confusion, "Did you guys make any extra stops?"

"No, we drove straight home," Benji replied. Miguel let out a strangely forced laugh. Causing Benji to pull back a bit in surprise.

"You must be the new doctor everybody is talking about," Brandy-Sue announced.

"Everybody?" Miguel mumbled, thinking it was strange the town was already talking about his husband after a few days.

"Oh, I didn't realize we had a guest," said Benji. Miguel stepped closer to Benji.

"Yes, This is Brandy-Sue, one of our new neighbors." Benji furrowed his brow.

"I didn't see any houses while driving to the manor." Miguel smiled.

"It's nice to meet you, Brandy-Sue," said Benji. Gideon nodded and walked past them.

"Hey, you wanted me to help you set up your study, right?" Miguel said, practically begging him with his eyes.

"No, no, that can wait." Benji grinned and shut the door behind him. He leaned down, kissed Miguel's forehead, and went upstairs. Miguel sighed and turned toward Brandy-Sue. "What are you guys doing for dinner?"

Dinner went slowly, with the kids talking over each other and Wyatt constantly getting up to pee. Brandy-Sue's husband worked late, which she said most likely meant he and his coworkers were at the local brewery. She talked the entire time. Glancing at his husband, Miguel could tell Benji now regretted his part in inviting her to dinner. Finally, she left, and Miguel forced Benji to go down into the basement with him to make up for his indiscretion.

"Well, she's a character," Benji said as they made their way down the wooden steps.

"More like a cartoon character," Miguel replied, holding onto his husband's arm. "Seriously, you inviting her means she will come by regularly from now on." Benji shrugged his shoulders.

"It seemed to help you pass the time. It was also good that she gave you a ride home."

"Yeah, our little Emma's got a temper on her," said Miguel.

"Maybe a little. Do you think it will become an issue?" They both rooted around, looking for some kind of light.

"You got called into school, so I'd say it already is." Miguel found the hanging string of the center basement light and tugged it, illuminating the room. "Wallah," he said as he saw the basement, packed with old furniture from a long-forgotten time. It smelled of old wood dust and something sour he could not pinpoint. Benji feigned clapping.

"Seems like you handled things pretty well, Peanut."

"You weren't there. I acted like a complete fool in front of that Principal Connor." Miguel shivered as he recalled the event.

"Oh, it couldn't have been that bad," said Benji.

"I'm sure when I started yelling at him, it got pretty bad."

Benji winced. "No. I'm sure he could tell you're just a passionate, caring parent." Miguel didn't buy it but appreciated the attempt. Benji was a master at making him feel better about his less-than-rational self. He watched as his husband lifted a chair and inspected it to see if it would suit his study. Miguel smiled, thinking how good he looked doing manual labor.

"Today has just been stressful. I could really use something to help with that," said Miguel, hoping Benji would notice.

"Yeah, I bet. You had a lot on your plate," Benji replied

"Yeah! Can you think of something that might relieve stress?" Miguel looked at his husband, trying to send the strongest signals he could.

"I can make us some lavender tea. Benji suggested, causing Miguel to appear defeated. *Crash*! A sound from the back of the basement alerted the two men.

"Oh great! Don't tell me we have rats now," said Miguel. Neither of them could find any signs of rodents. When they were satisfied, they grabbed the few pieces of furniture and made their way back upstairs. When Miguel realized he had forgotten to turn off the light, he made it halfway down the stairs before the bulb clicked itself off.

Chapter 11

A convenience store on the edge of town remained one of the last lit-up buildings of the night. A dutiful employee swept the porch one last time before Betty Crawford, the kind elderly woman who owned the shop, walked onto the porch to lock up the ice freezer just as she had for the last thirty years.

"Jason, you go ahead, finish up, and head home. I'll close up tonight," she said. Jason put the broom down and looked at her.

"You sure, Ma'am? I don't mind staying."

"You go on and enjoy your youth. Lord knows I didn't spend enough time doing that myself." Jason smiled at her, took off his apron, hung it up in the back of the store, and grabbed his stuff. As he was rushing out the front door to his car, Betty shouted, "Be sure to say hello to your mother for me; I look forward to seeing her in church on Sunday!" Jason gave her a quick nod and then drove off toward town.

Betty stood there a moment, taking in the quiet scene that her shop near the woodline provided. She would usually have delighted in the chorus of sounds nature gave her on any given night. But that night, she was deafened by the quiet. A quiet that would only seem natural in a soundproof booth. It was discomforting, but she shook it off and returned to the task of closing her shop. Betty was at a point in her life when she needed a cane to get around. Some of the tasks required to complete the day needed a bit more effort from her than her young employee, but she would never admit it. Betty would take her time and close it the same way she used to with her husband. The previous week, she had trouble focusing even though she prided herself on her razor-sharp mind. However, this week, she felt as though a cloud surrounded her thoughts. She would lose track of time and become seemingly oblivious to her surroundings. Her family was concerned, but she did her best to reassure them. She was old but not ready to be senile. Besides, the fogginess didn't really upset her. It was the sounds in her head that replaced the silence of her surroundings. She couldn't shake off a feeling of being watched, though it never came to anything.

Creek.

Betty had finished counting the money in the drawers when she looked up surprised, hearing what sounded like someone stepping onto the porch. "Hello." She received no reply. "We are closed, please come back tomorrow." Still, no response. She placed her hand on the shotgun concealed under the counter. The town was generally safe, but she wasn't taking any chances. The sound of steps continued, becoming progressively louder as they reached the entrance where the front door was propped open. Betty pointed the shotgun toward the sound. At that point, the footsteps that would have revealed the mute stranger suddenly stopped their creaking approach. A few moments passed, and Betty was unsure if the person was still waiting outside the door. She thought about calling out once more when the TV in the backroom came on, playing a rerun of Jeopardy. She spun around. For a moment, her mind was filled with panic, and her heart raced a mile per minute. Then, in a single moment, she felt calm.

Her tight grip on the shotgun loosened, and she placed it on the counter. She walked around the counter and moved toward the front door with her cane one step ahead. When she reached the doorway, a gust blew by, sending an unnatural shiver through her, and that is when she heard the voice. She dropped her cane and walked into the woods, following the sound of singing.

***

Wyatt was startled awake. His head throbbed, and his chest felt as if an elephant was sitting on it. He couldn't understand what he had seen in his dream. Who was that lovely lady? Why was she walking into the woods? For a long time, he lay looking up at the stars Miguel had stuck on his ceiling. The intense beating of his heart slowed, and his eyes began to feel heavy once again. He reached down to pull his blanket back up to his chest and started to drift back to sleep. He felt the weight of the blanket hanging off the bed, causing it to start slipping back down. He grabbed handfuls of fabric, tugging it back onto the bed. He rolled onto his side and closed his eyes. Still, the tingling sensation of the material sliding against his skin caused his eyes to shoot open. He froze, fear creeping into every inch of his tiny body.

The blanket slid slowly down past his chest, his stomach, and then his knees. The fear of being fully exposed was enough to send him grasping at the blanket before it left his feet. He held onto it with both hands. Wyatt grunted, forcefully pulling back to yank the blanket onto the bed. His body trembled, and his arms grew weak. Suddenly, the blanket was aggressively stripped from him and flew across the room, hitting the wall. Wyatt shrieked and darted for the door. His short leg, without its brace, wabbled as he stumbled through the doorway.

Darting to Gideon's room, he knew if he could reach his brother, he would be safe. He just had to find Gideon's door with what little light the moon shining through the window at the end of the hall gave him. Tears trickled down his cheek, and he trembled, willing himself to move faster than his leg would allow. Darkness crept up behind him like a shadow, threatening to engulf him. Despite the pain of his bad leg hitting the floor, he pressed forward. That's when he found it, the last door on the left. He grabbed the handle and pushed it open, letting out a scream.

His brother bolted out of bed. "Wyatt! What's wrong?" Gideon looked him over, just like he did anytime Wayt was hurt. Through the mess of tears and labored breathing, Wyatt tried to explain.

"Nice lady, walk into wood. And, someone singing, and my blanket pulled off me." He pressed himself into his brother and sobbed.

"Bad dream?" Gideon sighed. "It's okay." He took Wyatt by the hand and led him out into the hall; they stood there for a moment. Wyatt looked down the hall to see if the shadow was still there. When he was satisfied that it had gone, he looked up at Gideon, who appeared to be staring out of the window. "Wyatt, do you see that?" Gideon looked down at Wyatt, who tried but was too small to see. He frowned, sinking back into his heels. Gideon looked back out the window and shook his head, "Oh, I thought I saw… a woman." He stood there for a moment, eyes scanning the yard before glancing down at Wyatt. "I guess we're both seeing things."

Gideon laughed it off and then walked Wyatt to his bedroom. When inside, Gideon made a big show of looking around, checking under the bed, the closet, and even the window. He then looked at Wyatt and gave him a big brother-approved nod before sitting on his bed. "Hey, bad dreams really suck. But you have to remember they are just in your head, okay?" Wyatt nodded. "Listen. I get bad dreams too, especially, well, especially since mom and dad passed." He took a seat on Wyatt's bed, "But have you ever noticed how bad dreams go on forever? You always wake up before they end."

"Mhm," replied Wyatt.

"Well, when you wake up, you can think of your own ending, you know? No one made any rules saying you can't."

"Okay."

"Okay. Now, get some rest. I will check on you tomorrow."

"Tuck me!" Wyatt said. Gideon picked the blanket up from the floor and proceeded to wrap it around Wyatt tight like he always did. Wyatt laughed and pretended to be trapped. When he was good and tucked in, Gideon turned off the lights, said goodnight one last time, and walked back into the hallway out of sight. For a moment, Wyatt was nervous. He looked around his room again, making sure nothing was different. Then, Wyatt turned onto his side, about to let himself be carried away back to sleep, but decided to look at his glow-in-the-dark stars one last time. He looked up, saw the green glowing stickers, and smiled. His smile quickly faded when, out of the corner of his eye, he saw star after star disappearing until a dark shadow consumed them all.

Chapter 12

Emma wove her way through the kids, heading for class. She took a deep breath and walked in. The noisy room hushed as she made her way to her seat. Kids whispered to one another, and some nervously scooted their chairs away from hers. She had expected to be swarmed by the other kids; she thought they might attack her. Instead, they appeared to be scared. Even Cindy, who, at that moment, was nursing the left side of her jaw, didn't even speak a word. Emma wasn't sure how to feel. She was like a thorny rose bush decorated with Christmas lights. Nobody could help looking at her, but they didn't touch her. If they had thought she was weak, they didn't anymore.

"Emma!" Channing's cracked voice called over the sea of children, "Emma, come over here!" She smiled and briskly walked over to her only friend. As usual, the class was unruly, and the kids ignored their teacher. The teacher got mad and made empty threats. Everyone pretended to understand why Washington crossing the Delaware mattered. The kids at the back weren't interested in history. Instead, they talked about the disappearance of Henry Winkler.

"I bet zombies got him," a boy with more freckles than face said.

"No! my mom said it was probably the government, the CAI," A girl with round glasses put forward.

Cindy, making sure her voice was heard, jutted out her chin. "CIA, Jenny, and none of that is true. He was a dumb lay about that died because he drank too much."

"Oh, what's a lay?" the freckled kid asked.

"That's what my mom calls my dad," a boy with long hair sitting further back said.

Cindy, trying her best to sound knowledgeable, said, "It means he was lazy." Emma found herself pulled toward their conversation and strained to hear the details. Channing scribbled on his notepad, seemingly lost in his head. After class broke for computer lab studies, Emma led Channing to a private place to talk.

"Do you know who Henry Winkler is?" Emma asked. Channing looked at her, confused. "The old handyman? He used to live three houses away from mine. He seemed really nice, always smelled like my dad did after working late."

"Did you hear about him disappearing?" Channing shifted from foot to foot, glancing over his shoulder. He is getting nervous about being late to the lab, Emma thought. "C'mon, what have you heard?"

"Only that no one can find him; he just vanished. His truck was left just outside town. The Sheriff hasn't ruled out an abduction."

"Wow, Channing, you know a lot," Emma said, impressed.

"I remember things real well, and my mom is a gossip." Channing smiled.

Chapter 13

Gideon walked through the enormous doors and exited the school. The air was cool and crisp, just as he liked it. He had gotten to know some of the kids already and was even invited to a house party that weekend. He didn't plan on going.

"Hey, how was school?" Benji asked while Gideon got comfortable in the front seat.

"It was okay. Where is Emma?" He noticed her absence right away. There was less movement and talking.

Benji cleared his throat and started the car. "Brandy-Sue drove her home," he laughed.

"Miguel's best friend."

"If she has it her way," Benji added. They drove through the school parking lot, but instead of taking a right, they took a left.

"Where are we going?"

Benji took a deep breath, his eyes still on the road ahead. "Well, actually... I thought I'd surprise you."

"A surprise?" Gideon tried not to look visibly worried. He knew that whatever it was, his uncle was simply trying to connect with him. That's when he saw it. Behind the driver's seat, partially stuffed underneath, was a bag filled with his old hockey gear. He recognized it instantly because it had a Boston Bruins patch sewn onto the bag. "Where are we going?" He tried to suppress his newfound anxiety.

"Oh, I um. Well, I heard that this little town has its very own hockey team. So, I thought, what better way for you to meet teens like you than through your favorite sport!"

"I have no problems making friends; you really shouldn't have Benji. I mean, I really appreciate the thought, but…."

"I know that you had to put a lot of things on hold to make this move. I wanted to show you that you can still be a kid, you know?" Gideon sunk in his seat. He wanted to scream and then possibly open the door and roll out. Yes, he loved playing hockey but was not ready to commit to something like that so soon.

However, seeing the effort his uncle was making, he felt unable to do anything. So, instead, he replied, "Thanks, Benji." He could tell that saying that meant more than he expected. Another turn and they were coming up on open fields with bleachers.

"This is the place," Benji said.

"Uh, I don't think so, Benji. This looks like a soccer field."

"Well, this is where the directions told me to go," Benji said, shrugging his shoulders. Gideon sat in confusion, trying to discover the thing that didn't feel right. Then his eyes widened when he realized something about the town. Gideon couldn't believe he hadn't thought of it before, but how did a place this small afford an ice rink? The realization of what he was walking into and how ill-prepared he was for it caused the feeling of nausea to pass. He looked over at his gear, designed for the cold weather, and then looked up as they parked beside the field. He could see boys his age running around with hockey sticks. RUNNING. They were playing field hockey. Something Gideon had never imagined playing in his lifetime.

"This place seems nice," Benji said as they got out of the van. Gideon cleared his throat.

"I'm going to find a bathroom. I'll be back." He quickly rushed off, and a familiar face approached Gideon, carrying a box filled with candy and other snacks.

"Miles!"

"Hey, I'm glad you decided to join the team. We could use some fresh blood."

"You work… concession," Gideon said, feeling disheartened.

"That, and I help keep the gear clean and make sure they have water," said Miles proudly. He handed a bag of something to an older man who was most likely one of the players' dads. The guy walked off, shaking his head, seemingly agitated. *Oh, great,* thought Gideon to himself. He had hoped he had an "in" with the other players. Instead, he was in with a free bag of skittles.

"Can you tell me anything about the other players? I figure you might have the inside scoop," Gideon said, trying to find the silver lining.

"Oh yeah, I know all the stats! But tryouts started 10 minutes ago." Gideon's face went pale. He spun around to find his uncle holding the bag with his gear. He was silently staring and judging the other kids shoveling candy and fried stuff they got from Miles down their throats. He was disgusted and rushed over to Benji.

"Hey! I'm late; I'm going to throw on my gear and head in." Gideon paused for a moment and pointed at the bleachers. "You can sit over there if you want." He couldn't help noticing Benji's smile.

Gideon rushed to put on his knee pads, grab his stick, and head toward the field. He made his way over to the other nervous-looking kids, who he assumed were trying out as well. The team was on the field running plays. "Put your name on the clipboard," A short, stout man with a round head and large mustache said. Gideon quickly jotted down his name and went to stand next to the other kids.

It wasn't long before they were made to run shooting drills. The concept was simple on paper. The coach would blow his whistle, and the first person in line would rush toward the goal and catch the puck, or ball in this case. Then, they would try to shoot into an empty net. The exercise proved challenging for many of them. The first one to try made a mad rush to where he would receive the ball but ended up missing the pass and turning a full 180 degrees, trying to recover it. The next boy was more timid, going so slow that the coach could have walked the ball to him. Eventually, the coach screamed, "There are only three periods in a game, kid! Pick it up; we don't have all day!"

That caused the boy to slip on the ball and fall over. He crawled to the back of the line in shame. A few more went with varying levels of success. One even got the ball to hit the goal post. When Gideon stepped up, Miles, who he assumed was taking an unscheduled break, perked up. Gideon looked up at the bleachers, saw Benji, and smiled. Then he looked at the coach and gave him a nod. Gideon, with his stick down, moved with haste to the center of the field. Despite the lack of skates and his leg brace, his legs were strong, and he was fast. With great ease and with no hesitation, he caught the ball with his stick and moved it down the field. In one swift motion, Gideon shot the ball into the left side of the goal. He figured it was a decent shot, but he couldn't help but notice that the coach had his eyebrows raised in surprise. Gideon ran by the other players, who seemed deflated. He saw that a few from the Green Hollow team watched from the side. One of them, with a C on his jersey, nodded at the coach. It was hard to make out what he looked like, but he had brown curly hair. The guy standing next to him was tall, with sandy-colored hair, and glared directly at Gideon. Gideon could feel the guy's dislike for him from any distance. He had dealt with this kind of attitude before, often.

It wasn't long before the trials were over. Gideon glanced up at his uncle, who was grinning from ear to ear, and gave him a nod that indicated he would soon make his way over.

"Good work out there, kid," the coach said as he passed by. Gideon grinned and followed the rest of the players to the lobby, knowing he must have made the cut. He didn't have much time to celebrate. He was met by Miles rushing over toward him, waving his arms enthusiastically. Next to Miles was a skinny kid in a black sweater whom Gideon had never met before.

"You killed it out there," Miles said. Gideon readjusted his bag on his shoulder. "Thanks."

"I'm sure you'll make the team. Anyway, this is Jason. He works at the convenience on the edge of town."

"Oh, hey! I haven't made my way there yet," said Gideon.

Jason frowned. "Don't bother. We're probably closing down now."

"Yeah, you sure?" Gideon asked.

"Yeah, Betty, the owner, disappeared last night. There was no sign of a break-in. The store was unlocked, and her cane was left on the floor; she never went anywhere without it," Miles told Gideon. Jason sighed. "She's a great boss. I'm going around asking for volunteers to help look for her. Even the mayor is helping out."

"I'm sorry to hear that. I'd love to help. Let me just tell my uncle."

It didn't take much for him to convince uncle Benji to let him help with the search. The three boys made their way to the edge of town where the convenience store was located. There, an older woman was standing on the store porch, yelling orders at the small crowd. She appeared to have a permanent furrow on her brow as if it was stuck from years of glaring at people. Next to her, standing off to the side, was what looked like the town sheriff. He wore a grizzled look and had a stubby beard and blue tattoos on his forearms. He had his arms crossed and tended to nod his head a lot at what the woman was saying.

"That's the mayor," Miles whispered. Gideon nodded and looked at the mayor. He was surprised at the authority she exuded despite her short stature. The boys moved up to the crowd.

"Alright, I want accountability on this one. Everyone has a buddy, and no one goes anywhere without them," Mayor Spruce said. "Stick to the areas I assigned. I want everybody here by sundown." She turned to the Sheriff, who nodded in agreement. As the crowd dispersed, Gideon saw Agatha with three other girls. As she turned to walk in the other direction, Gideon couldn't help but think how pretty she was. He felt his cheeks warm and tried to shake it off.

"You alright, Gideon?" miles asked.

"Yeah, looks like everybody has already gotten started. We better join a group," Gideon replied.

"How bout that one?" Jason asked, pointing at Agatha's group.

"Sure," Gideon agreed, trying to keep his cool.

"Oh, won't you just put that silly thing down already, Carl!"

Gideon twisted his head, recognizing the two older men he had seen in the town arguing.

"Don't you get on to me now, Roy! We might need a good flashlight," Carl snapped back.

"In daylight? You got dropped on your head too many dang times," Roy said. The corner of Gideon's mouth twisted into a grin.

"Gideon!" Miles yelled from the group of girls, "Come on, man! You're holding things up!" Gideon noticed Agatha looking at him and jogged toward the group. He smiled sheepishly as he arrived.

"Sorry, guys."

Deep in the forest, Gideon, Agatha, and Miles walked around together. The other two girls with Agatha were called over to a different group. Miles had not stopped talking since they entered the woods, and it was beginning to wear thin on Gideon. He tried to put on a polite smile, but with time, that faded. "So everyone figures that trees are separate plants that don't and have much to do with each other," said Miles.

"Uh huh," replied Gideon.

"But actually, they communicate between themselves with their roots!"

"Okay."

"And those roots, get this, are connected to something called a mycelium network. Do you know what that is?"

"No, but I'm sure you're going to tell me," Gideon replied. For a moment, Miles looked deflated and stopped his chattering. Gideon couldn't help but feel a tinge of guilt.

"Well, what is it?" Agatha suddenly chimed in.

That brought Miles back. "Fungi, or mushrooms as you may know them," said Miles, twisting his head and gasping. "Look over there; that pine over there has a huge Saprophytic fungus on it!" He rushed over out of earshot. Gideon sighed and looked at Agatha, who had a severe look on her face.

"What?" Gideon asked.

"You didn't have to be rude, you know," Agatha said.

"I wasn't trying to be."

"It appears you're pretty good at it."

They shared a silent moment together before Gideon said, "I'm sorry for the other day, you know?"

"Me too. Not a great first impression, huh?"

"Yeah, I'm generally good with those."

Agatha rolled her eyes but smiled, "About Miles. You know he means well. He has some odd hobbies, but he means well."

Gideon looked over at Miles, who was jumping up and down, trying to grab the mushroom, "Yeah, he's a character, alright."

"He just grew up differently. He only has his dad and that guy there, who is old enough to be his grandpa."

"Oh, so nearly in his grave."

"He's pretty spry for an old guy, actually." They laughed before turning to Miles.

"Hey, Miles, Aren't we supposed to be looking for someone?" asked Gideon.

"Oh, yeah, right," Miles replied and then ran back to them. They continued searching but turned up nothing.

Chapter 14

Miguel set out to accomplish the impossible. He wanted to clean and set up each of the rooms downstairs in such a way that no one would ever think the house had been abandoned for a hundred years. He started in the kitchen, placing every dish, bowl, cup, and other utensil in its special place. He scrubbed every counter and cabinet until he was down on both knees, cleaning the floor.

It had taken several hours, but the job was done, and Miguel was able to look at it with pride. For a moment, he convinced himself that he was made for this work. His pride switched to horror when a four-year-old tyrant named Wyatt came marching into the kitchen, throwing open the freshly cleaned cabinets in search of a "snack." Snack was a word that Miguel would learn Wyatt held in a sacred place in his limited vocabulary, only second to "No" and barely ahead of "Sippy." Miguel had learned that reasoning with the toddler was about as practical as reasoning with a wild cat. Trying not to react to the greasy handprints that had already undone his work, he tried his best to reason with Wyatt and ask him to wait until dinner. That, of course, gave Wyatt the opportunity to combine his three favorite words into the broken sentence, "NO! I want snack and sippy!" Wyatt then punctuated his point by grabbing a bag of flour and doing his best impression of a white Christmas. Eventually, Miguel caved and gave Wyatt his snack and sippy. Then, he cleaned the kitchen for another hour.

Once done, he turned his attention to the front parlor, which he had set up earlier that day with the antique furniture they had found in the basement. He had thought to himself how impressed he was that the chairs were still in good condition after so long. He already found himself preferring one armchair in particular. The very one that Wyatt was jumping on while making his best attempt to shove as many cookies in his mouth as possible. Crumbs went everywhere. Wyatt continued to bounce while pointing to a lovely blown-glass bowl that Miguel had purchased in France, "I made Potion!" Wyatt proudly exclaimed.

"Potion?" Miguel's eyes widened, and his jaw dropped several inches when he realized that the potion that Wyatt had pointed to was a mixture of dirt, sippy, and crayons all mushed together.

"Off the chair, Wyatt!"

"No!"

"Wyatt! You need to listen to me; I need you to."

"No!" Wyatt stood on one of the chair arms, and Miguel could hear the ripping of threads from his weight pulling against the fabric. He rushed over to Wyatt and snatched him up around the waist, putting him over by the "potion." Then, he ran over to the chair to brush off the crumbs. *Crash.*

The sound of the bowl hitting the ground made Miguel shriek. Wyatt, being unable to handle the weight of his potion, had allowed it to spill onto the rug. Another antique.

"Que me trajo dios? Porque me castiga, Señor?" Miguel screamed in his native tongue before switching back to English and saying, "Can you just stop being such a nuisance for one minute so I can enjoy a moment of peace?" Suddenly, the tyrant morphed back into a four-year-old boy as tears weld up in his eyes. He looked at Miguel with a pitiful expression, quivering lip and all.

"You're mean!" he yelled as he ran past him. Miguel cleaned up the shattered bowl and began cleaning the rug the best he could. The anger he felt was replaced slowly with guilt for how he had reacted. With a deep sigh, Miguel stood back up and decided to find Wyatt. He remembered how much it meant to him whenever his father would apologize to him as a kid.

"Wyatt!" he shouted as he entered the foyer. He looked inside Grandpa's room, where the old man was taking a nap. Mary had gone out to buy a few things. She generally kept to herself, which he didn't mind, but it made the house seem empty during the day whether she was there or not. "Wyatt, come here, please." There was no response. *SLAM.*

The sound of a door slamming upstairs reverberated through the foyer, instantly drawing Miguel's attention. His head snapped in that direction. His mind raced with ideas of what Wyatt could be breaking. He went upstairs to find him. Halfway up the stairs, Miguel thought he could hear something rolling against the hardwood floor toward the end of the hallway. He made his way to the top and looked over, seeing nothing.

"Wyatt, I hope you are not breaking anything up here!" The rolling sound repeated. Miguel realized it must be coming from the room at the end of the hallway. "Wyatt?" With no reply, Miguel made his way down the hall. He shivered as the temperature dropped unexpectedly. Miguel wondered if the heating failed to make it this far. He held himself as he continued forward. Once he reached the door to Gideon's room, he stopped and listened through the closed door. He wanted to be sure he was correct before invading the kid's privacy. When he heard the sound again, he opened the door, expecting a small child getting into mischief. But when he looked inside, there was nothing. He walked in and stood in the middle of the room.

"Wyatt, Come out! You shouldn't be in your brother's room."

Miguel looked under the bed and in the closet but found no sign of Wyatt. He was about to leave when he heard the rolling sound again. This time, it was faint. He followed the sound until he reached the wall shared by the adjacent room. He placed his ear to the wall to hear. *BANG.*

Miguel jumped backward. Something had slammed into the wall. With little hesitation, he rushed out of Gideon's room to the one next door. He threw open Emma's door and peered into the dark room. In the far right corner, he saw a lump beneath Emma's blanket.

"Wyatt, You don't need to hide." Miguel noticed movement under the sheets that confirmed Wyatt's presence. He moved closer, extending his left arm to grip the blanket.

"Miguel?" Wyatt said from the doorway behind him. Frozen, his arm was inches away from the blanket. He did not dare turn away; a frigid cold moved throughout his body. His heart pounded aggressively against his ribcage. His fingers were unsure how to act. Miguel took a deep breath, gripped Emma's blanket, and threw it off the bed. Nothing. He should have been relieved, but instead, he felt uneasy.

"Why you Emma's room?"

Miguel turned sharply toward Wyatt. "Let's go downstairs." He grabbed Wyatt and rushed down the stairs. Just as he arrived at the end of the stairway, the front door opened. Benji walked in with Gideon close behind. They stopped in the hallway. Miguel cleared his throat, sat Wyatt down, and ran a hand through his hair to smooth it back down. The last thing he wanted was for them to think he was going crazy.

"Everything okay?" Benji asked. Miguel did his best to suppress the bubble of irritation rising inside him. Of course, things weren't okay.

"Yeah, everything's great," he said, patting Wyatt's head. "I was just playing with Wyatt."

"Where's Emma?" Gideon asked.

"Still with Brandy-Sue. She should be home soon," Miguel replied.

"Miguel in Emma room," Wyatt blurted.

"I was looking for you, silly," Miguel said, forcing a smile. "Speaking of Brandy-Sue, she invited us to the brewery tonight."

"Who would watch the kids?" asked Benji, shutting the door behind him.

"I could," Gideon said.

"That works." Miguel didn't hesitate. He figured Gideon was used to watching them and needed a drink.

A few hours later, he had his hair slicked back and was closing the last few buttons on his dress shirt when there was a knock at the door. He was thankful they wouldn't be pulling up in the old minivan. Brandy-Sue could be annoying, but if he were honest with himself, he was excited and even looking forward to their conversation.

"Ready?" Benji asked. He leaned over and kissed Miguel's forehead, adding, "You look perfect."

"Yes… and I know." He grabbed his black coat and his husband's hand, practically pulling him down the stairs.

***

The Green Hallow Brewery was a center piece of the town, along with the old boot. It was a busy night, with people standing in every corner of the wooden building. Inside, it smelled of hops, and the patrons were energetic. Everyone seemed to be happy to be there. Even Miguel could feel a smile form on his face as if the energy were contagious. Brandy-Sue led their group to a table at the back, passing a long bar. Behind the bar, a doorway showed the enormous machines that produced the town's famous beer. When they arrived at their table, a waitress appeared out of thin air, ready to take their drink order. Initially, Miguel had intended to have a beer and take it slow. However, the light feeling the place gave encouraged him to order a selection of beers to try. Meanwhile, Benji went from his usual glass of light beer to a whole pint of amber ale. Miguel convinced himself that it was just because of the stress they had been under, but a small voice told him not to worry so much and relax.

"Isn't this place great?" Brandy-Sue asked rhetorically.

"Yes, I love the atmosphere," Benji replied.

"This place is magical, lots of fun for the town. I've been coming here for years now." Joe Hidecker said, surprising Miguel and Benji. Joe had only spoken two words the whole car ride there, but suddenly, he couldn't be stopped, "I have stock in this company; they are going international, you know? The wife and I might renew our vows here." Brandy-Sue nodded in agreement, speaking a lot less, almost as if giving her husband a turn for once. Joe had transformed into an expressive and charismatic character, telling stories and jokes while kicking back drinks.

Meanwhile, his wife seemed to be calmer and more subdued. Miguel looked down and noticed the food and drink had been replenished. He couldn't remember ordering more. He looked around to see where the ninja servers were coming from but to no avail. As he looked, Miguel couldn't help but notice an odd couple at the bar who appeared to be arguing. A short old woman with grey hair in a suit sat next to a plump ginger man with a more colorful style of pants and jacket. The man took a big swig from his mug and noticed Miguel staring his way. He put his beer t down and pointed at Miguel, which caused the older woman to turn and face them. Miguel suddenly felt the urge to run and hide. She had intense eyes that made Miguel feel guilty without knowing why. The two older folks stood up and made their way to

Miguel's table. Miguel squeezed Benji's arm until he noticed. When they were at the table, a hush came over everyone. The older woman was the first to speak.

"So, is everyone having a pleasant time tonight?"

"Yes, Mayor Spruce," Joe replied, "Just enjoying another excellent brew tonight with our new neighbors."

"Ah yes, the new tenants of the manor. I have been meaning to make a trip up there for some time. I hope you two are settling in okay."

"We are," Benji replied. "Nice of you to check in on us."

"Are things going well there? No disturbances?"

"No, everything is good. It's a beautiful house," said Miguel.

"It is a nice house. I once tried to buy it myself, but your father wouldn't budge. How is he doing these days?" Miguel suddenly felt uneasy at her probing. That's when he noticed the man with her watching him carefully.

"He is doing pretty good," Benji replied.

"Enough of all that, I'm Brenden, the owner of this little place. Can I get you guys a round of our seasonal ale on the house?" Before they had a chance to answer, a server appeared seemingly out of nowhere with a tray. She sat it in the center of the table. Miguel couldn't believe it; this was the best service he had ever had. Brenden smiled down at them, red-faced and jolly.

"Enjoy, and if there is anything you need, don't hesitate to seek me out," Brenden said, wiggling his finger at them. "Now, if you'll excuse me, it's been a whole thirty minutes since anyone has danced." The sound of a flute and violin erupted throughout the building. Brenden grabbed hold of a random woman's arm and hoisted her into the middle of the floor, where they began to dance a folk-like jig. Their inspiration sent several people scattering to join them in the fun. Everyone laughed, and some clanked their drinks on the table in rhythm with the music. Brendon moved in a light, airy manner despite his size.

"Bunch of fools," the Mayor mumbled, walking back toward her seat at the bar. A dancer stumbled too close to her; she shoved him out of her way without hesitation. Miguel felt that the mayor was not someone to cross.

Chapter 15

"Here, take these. I got more than one." Emma said, handing Channing plastic fangs, she dug from her pocket. He raised an eyebrow but slipped the fangs into his mouth.

"Thanks." As he spoke, he drooled from his mouth and quickly rubbed it away. "My dad once told me someone sharpened their teeth to look like fangs. He said they were stupid," said Channing.

"My actual vampire teeth will grow in one day; these are just for training," Emma said.

"More bubbles!" Wyatt yelled from the bathroom.

"You don't need more bubbles; you need to finish and get ready for bed," Gideon yelled back.

"Bubbles!"

Emma, hearing this, said, "There, my brother is busy; let's go outside!"

"Outside? Emma, that is kind of dangerous, right?" said Channing.

"We have to go outside because vampires go out at night. What kind of vampires stay inside?"

"Ones with allergies to most plant life."

A thud was heard from the bathroom, and a limping four-year-old in his birthday suit came in full view of Emma and Channing. He supported his weight on his more muscular leg and giggled at his sister without shame. He limped away as Gideon ran after him with his brace clutched in one hand and the other reaching out to grab him.

Emma rolled her eyes. "Brothers." She leaned around the corner to make sure that her bothers were gone before turning to Channing. "Now's the time!" They darted down the stairs, past Grandpa, who was sitting in his chair in the front parlor, and ran out the front door. The cold air stung her arms, but she wasn't going back inside for a jacket. Nope. It was time to explore and put her vampire training to good use. Almost immediately, her eyes found the great wall of trees lining the forest. She adjusted her fangs and took off.

"Wait! We aren't going in there at night. Monsters live there!" Channing said, stopping abruptly.

"That's what these are for," she pointed at her plastic fangs, "Can't be scared of monsters when you are one." She teased. Both Vampire kids stood outside the thick woods. Despite Emma's big talk, she was a little more hesitant to be the first one to enter the dark. They glanced at each other a few times, sharing smiles, then stared forward.

"What is that?" Channing suddenly asked, pointing into the forest. Emma's eyes were instantly drawn to a bright light that floated. It moved nimbly between trees, producing an amber glow.

"Maybe a firefly?" Emma stepped forward, her fears melted by her new curiosity.

"That's a big firefly then," Channing replied, following her. They entered, walking toward the bright light until two more orbs floated next to the first one. As they came closer, Emma realized the orbs were way bigger than any firefly she had seen in her life, moving swiftly and purposefully. They inched closer to the spheres until they entered a small clearing. *Crack.* Channing stepped on a branch, causing the orbs to fly high into the treetops. Emma raced to catch another glimpse of them, but they had vanished.

"Dang it, Channing!"

"I'm sorry."

"It's fine." Emma looked around, "Channing, do you remember how we got here?" The kids shared a look of terror as they attempted to recognize anything around them. Emma furrowed her brow and tried to think how long they had been walking. Channing fell to his knees and began to panic.

"Oh no! Oh no, why did we do that? We are so lost, Emma!" He began to tear up. Emma couldn't help but feel annoyed by her friend, then bad for getting them stuck in the first place.

"We are fine, Channing; we just have to take a moment to remember which way to go."

"If we go the wrong way, we could be lost in these woods forever, Emma. My dad told me once that these woods cross three different states." He continued crying, his face covered in snot and tears.

Emma sat down with him to think, "I wish we had a trail to follow back." Something bright above them caught the children's attention. A glow like a bright fire illuminated them from above. When Emma looked up, her eyes widened.

"Channing, Channing look!." Channing looked up and instantly stopped crying. They both stood up as what looked like a hundred amber-colored orbs of light floated down from the treetops and began to dance around them. Upon seeing this, both Emma and Channing were filled with joy and began to laugh and cheer at the spectacle before them. They jumped around and danced and played until they both fell down exhausted. Then all the lights stopped at once, and one that Emma, for some reason, knew was the one she had followed into the woods floated toward her. It was too bright to look at directly, but Emma reached out her hand.

"Will you help us?" she asked.

The orb came to rest in her hand, giving off a warm feeling that went through her whole body. Then, a voice she had never heard before entered her head.

It said, "Beware the banshee song. It took two; it will take three more." Emma had little time to react. All the lights flew into a line that led through the trees. Emma grabbed Channing, who was still mesmerized and gaping at the lights, by the hand. Channing looked surprised as she looked at him, smiling so her plastic fangs showed.

"Let's go." She broke through the trees, instantly feeling lighter and drawing in deep breaths of fresh air. Just as she felt relieved, her eyes found a small figure in the garden just beneath the large statue of a woman kneeling. The statue was wrapped in layers of stone fabric with her hands stretched outward. Resting in her palm was what appeared to be a large ornate bracelet. She looked down toward the ground, where Wyatt slept in his firefighter pajamas with his knees tucked into his chest. Emma rushed toward him with Channing hot on her heels. "Wyatt?" The moon hung low in a cloudless night sky, easily exposing her brother's body curled beneath the chipped, mossy statue. His wild red hair made his face that much paler, and for a moment, she feared he wasn't breathing.

"Wyatt!" This time, she yelled, dropping to her knees and shaking him vigorously.

Wyatt stirred, and his eyes fluttered open. "Emma?" She had little time to comprehend the look of confusion in his eyes because the sound of squeaky brakes sent a shiver of panic through her. Her Uncles were home. The car door opened just as Gideon flew through the front entrance.

"What's going on here?" Benji asked.

"Busted," Channing whispered.

Chapter 16

"And your brother was sleeping in the garden?" Miles repeated, walking with his hands gripping his backpack.

"Yeah, two kids running around in the woods and another sleeping under a statue." Gideon sighed, "It painted one hell of a scene." He pushed the school's front door open. It was a bright day with the usual hustle and bustle of kids running to get to their parent's cars or catch the bus. Gideon and Miles took a seat on the school steps.

"That's wild; how much trouble did that get you in?" Miles asked.

"Well, I still get to play hockey, but I'm on a probation kind of thing. Benji and Miguel lectured me for almost an hour."

"That's it? I'm surprised you still have your head! My pops would have taken everything from me for sure."

"Yeah, well, being an orphan still keeps me out of trouble right now." Gideon smiled so that Miles knew he could laugh at that. "Anyway, what are we doing before practice today?"

"Wow, you really did get out of it pretty clear, huh?"

"I'm an orphan, Miles. My new parental figures are trying their best, but they don't know much about disciplining a teenager."

"Well, I thought about maybe checking out the comic shop to see if anything interesting came in."

Gideon winced. "You really are a nerd."

"Hey man, when you live in a small town surrounded by woods, you can forgive a little escapism." The comic shop was not far from the field, so Gideon could think of little reasons to not check it out with his friend. They walked along the sidewalks until they reached the shops in the town square. Gideon focused so much on hockey that he had given little room for other hobbies. Miles, on the other hand, made a hobby of collecting hobbies. "Dude, you have to check out Furutsu Basuketto. I read the whole series in two nights, and I think it is way underrated!" Miles said emphatically.

Gideon shook his head, pretending to be interested but feeling uncomfortable after having watched one of his friend's suggested shows about a girl that turned into a cat and fell in love with other cats. He hadn't been able to look at Miles the same way since. Fortunately, the subject was dropped as the shop came into sight. The comic shop, named Epic Rolls, was a small one-story building with comic books lining the walls and a few small tables sitting in the middle, occupied by kids playing a card game. Gideon did his best to stay out of the way and let his friend nerd out for a bit. He was in his own head about hockey stunts. Then, out of the corner of his eye, he saw Agatha walking across the street. He made a quick move outside the store and did his best impression of someone not caring about a girl walking toward him. As Agatha began to walk in the other direction, Gideon suddenly felt words coming out of his mouth before he had time to think of anything.

"Give any history lessons today?" he asked.

Agatha stopped and turned around, "Well, a local Podunk historian's job is never done. I was just about to head over to my cousin's place and accept his proposal of marriage," she said. They both laughed.

"Well, he better be willing to pay your incredibly high dowry," Gideon continued.

"Oh, you almost made the mistake of complimenting me," she replied, "What are you doing around here anyway?" she asked.

"Just waiting for Miles." Gideon noticed she was fiddling with another stone, only this one was different. It was a deep red gem hanging from a thin silver chain.

"That's a cool rock," he said, instantly regretted pointing at her chest.

"Oh, this stone? It's a red quartz." She held it up and moved closer to him. "It's for strength and protection." As the awkward exchange took place, Miles appeared from the shop carrying a large black bag and smiling from ear to ear.

"I only came in for the latest issue, but then I saw that it came in three other variants and had to have them, too," Miles announced before noticing Agatha. Gideon sighed and looked away. He felt the heat rise in his face.

"Hey, Agatha!" Miles looked confused by his friend's bashful behavior, "You two getting along all right?"

"Oh yeah, perfectly," Gideon replied. He couldn't help but notice her smile a little at that.

"So, what are you two up to?" Agatha asked.

"Just hanging out before practice, trying to kill some time, you know," Gideon replied.

Miles shook his bag above his head, "Time well spent." Gideon saw, from the corner of his eye, two guys in their field hockey jerseys walking toward them from the direction of the hockey field. He turned, surprised to see them.

"You guys finished practice? Miles yelled.

"Yeah, well, the coach got some sort of stomach bug last night, so it's canceled," the boy with the C on his jersey said.

"Oh, the same bug he caught the last time he went out all night?" Miles replied.

"That's the one." He stopped in front of Gideon.

"Too bad, I wanted to see if last time was a fluke," his tall friend added. His attempt at antagonizing him fell short.

"Guess you'll have to wait till next time." The two of them continued walking. When they were out of earshot, Gideon turned to Miles.

"So you know those two pretty well?"

"Of course! That's Ricky, the team captain, and his friend Daniel. Both been playing hockey for a long time here." There was a moment of silence before Miles broke it. "So Agatha, what has you out and about today?"

"I'm meeting my mom here. She was picking up some supplies for her job."

"Oh, what does your mom do?"

"She's a nurse. She works with geriatrics."

Gideon's ears perked up as he realized something about what she had said. "Geriatrics? She works with older people?"

"That's what it means," Agatha replied

Before Gideon could make the connection, Mary, his grandpa's caretaker, walked up to Agatha and gave her a side hug and a kiss on the cheek in front of the boys, much to her daughter's embarrassment.

"Hey, Mom," she said in a hushed tone.

"Agi, I didn't know you knew Gideon." Gideon was taken aback, but he could clearly see the resemblance between them.

"I didn't know you knew him, Mom."

"Yeah, she looks after my grandpa," Gideon interjected, enjoying the sudden bout of shyness from Agatha.

"Y'all act surprised that everyone knows each other in a small town," Miles said.

"Well, what are you boys up to?"

"Practice was canceled, so we were just figuring that out ourselves."

Mary adjusted the bags in her arms and looked at her watch. "Well, I'm on my way to the manor now if you want a ride, Gideon."

"That would be awesome," Miles said, accepting the ride that wasn't offered to him. "It would be great to finally get a tour of that haunted palace," he said, elbowing Gideon.

Gideon shook his head, "Yeah, you can come too if you'd like 'Agi.'" He could see she was visibly annoyed by her nickname.

"Well, I was already planning to help my mom anyway. So sure."

Gideon was happy the ride was over after being smushed in the back with Agatha on the other side and Miles in the middle. Mary had too many supplies on the front passenger, and Gideon was too polite to try and get her to move them. Both Agatha and he were perfectly content with staring out their windows in silence, but Miles kept egging them to talk more. Once out of the car and after helping Mary take her supplies inside, the three went to the parlor. Miles didn't try to hide his excitement as he moved around the room, taking in every inch of Victorian decoration.

"Oh, hey," Miguel said, coming from the other end of the room. "We have company?"

"Yes, this is my friend, Miles," Gideon said.

"And this is my daughter I was telling you about, Agatha. It seems she already knows Gideon," added Mary.

Miguel wiggled his eyebrows at Gideon as he shook his head. He couldn't help smiling.

"How is Emory doing?" Mary asked, sorting through her supplies.

Miguel sighed. "Between him and Wyatt, I have my hands full."

"One of those days." She grabbed her bag and headed toward Emory's door. "I'll get him in a better mood."

"And I'm going to show them around our very haunted house." He said, lowering his voice in as creepy a way as he could muster. He laughed at himself, but it soon fizzled out when he noticed Miguel stiffen. He could have sworn that the color faded from his face. "I'm joking."

"Ha, yeah. Well, you kids have fun. If you need me, I'll be in the kitchen," said Miguel, walking briskly from the room.

Gideon thought the interaction odd but shook it off as he began walking his friends around the house. Miles made occasional ooh and aah sounds as Gideon made up historical facts about the manor.

"Now, this wall was built out of the same wood as the Mayflower, probably." Gideon threw his arms up exaggeratedly as they walked. "Over here, you may be able to spot the famous wallpaper used in French torture chambers in the 1600s." Gideon couldn't help but notice how much he enjoyed making Agatha smile and laugh at his silly *facts*. "The French didn't even need tools; the color was torture enough." That made Agatha burst out laughing and snorting.

They had made their way upstairs when Miles was quick to start opening doors and looking through rooms. Gideon worried about his family's privacy and ran after him as Miles went straight into Wyatt's room. "This must be your room, right?" Agatha asked, seeing all the toddler toys scattered about.

"Guys, let's get out of my LITTLE brothers' room," said Gideon.

Miles motioned toward Wyatt's closet. "That's a weird toy for a toddler." The three of them huddled together outside the small closet. Gideon picked up the old box, noticing the carvings all over it. Touching it gave him a strange feeling, a feeling he could not place.

"Should we open it?" asked Agatha.

Gideon, for some odd reason, felt like he shouldn't as if opening it would open something else. The pressure of his friend's eyes on him made his hand carefully move to open it anyway. However, when he did, he didn't expect only to find one lonely old picture. He exhaled a sigh of relief. The relief was short-lived as his eyes became fixated on the single photo. At first glance, it was nothing out of the ordinary. It was just an old-fashioned picture of two people wearing old-fashioned clothes. But Gideon found himself becoming more and more focused on it.

The man in the picture had a gruff expression under his thick beard. He wore a suit with tails and a top hat. The man was someone who clearly wanted people to see his wealth and status. He had his right hand tucked away inside his coat jacket and the left hand holding a woman's hand. Gideon made the connection that they were most likely married. The woman wore a softer expression that matched her more dressed-down look. She was wearing a simple white silk dress and pearls. Gideon thought she was very kind-looking. He momentarily thought of his own mother while looking at her. His eyes were then drawn to her jewelry. Something that seemed almost out of place with her wardrobe. She wore a metal bracelet with a green jewel at its center. It seemed ancient, even in such an old photo. Gideon Flinched. It was a black-and-white photo; how did he know it was green? Gideon looked at the bracelet again and noticed it was grey, matching the rest of the picture.

"Gideon?" Miles looked nervously at Agatha and back to Gideon, "You okay, buddy?"

Agatha touched Gideon's shoulder. "Hey!"

Gideon was startled. "Sorry, I'm sorry. I just got sort of zoned out there."

Chapter 17

Zechariah Baker pulled into his driveway and turned off his old truck like he had been doing for fifteen years now. The sun sank behind the thick wall of trees beside him, and he glared at it bitterly. Zechariah was thirsty and tired and thought he'd better not hear that woman rattle off at him tonight. He slammed his truck door shut and spat on the gravel that crunched beneath his oiled work boots. The house was quiet. Good. He headed straight for the couch, sitting back and plopping his feet onto the freshly cleaned table. He turned on the TV.

"Kate, where's dinner?" He shook his head. She had been stripping away at his nerves this last week. He couldn't stand the sight of her.

"Here," she said, sitting his plate and a beer in front of him. He didn't bother looking at her. He didn't want to see that pathetic wounded animal look on her face or the black eye she seemed to rub in his. He stared intently at the TV, hoping she would fade back out of the room. But she stood there.

"She called again." Kate barely had time to duck out of the way of the beer bottle as it was flung at her head but crashed and shattered on the wall.

Zechariah stood up, "You just shut it, Kate. I already see where this is going. You are so naggy, you know? What, I can't have a social life no more? What kind of life do I have going on here?" He spat on the carpet. Kate stood there with her jaw clenched. She never reacted to his comments anymore. Unfortunately for her, that only made him angrier. He sat back down and started picking at his food, "Barren woman can't make a kid and can't even make a decent meal."

"That isn't my fault, Zack," she reacted. He knew the kid thing would make her say something.

"Ha! You are as barren as they come! I married a nothing that can't even do the one thing women are made to do!" He continued to pick at his food until he felt a strange fog enter his mind. He tried to shake it off and, with a growl, stood up and walked to the kitchen to grab another beer.

"You won't let me get checked. I need to see a doctor. Maybe they can help me, or maybe…maybe they can help you." At that, Zechariah slammed the fridge door and grabbed Kate by the back of her head, dragging her into the living room. He lifted her up, taking a swig of his beer while she tried desperately to get him to release his grip.

"There ain't nothing wrong with me. Nothing! You got that, Kate?" He didn't notice letting Kate go or that the front door was suddenly open. That fog just kept creeping into his skull. He didn't realize how long he had stood there or that his wife was now pointing a shotgun at his head.

"What are you doing, Kate?" he asked, still trying to work through the fog, "Put that thing down."

"Shut up! Just Shut up, Zack!" she screamed, shaking the weapon at him. "You don't let me get checked, and then you go around sleeping with anyone who'll let you."

"Put the gun down, Kate!" Usually, he would have been able to grab her, but his head made it hard to keep track of what was happening.

"No! You listen to me now! I've put up with too much for the last fifteen years!" Zechariah started to approach her. "Not another step! Not one more step, or I will blow your head off!"

"Kate, you know you ain't got it in you to pull that trigger. Now put it down." She wouldn't budge, "I SAID PUT IT DOWN!" Zechariah was frozen in place. Suddenly, his posture relaxed, and his eyes glossed over. Kate looked at him, confused. Without a word, Zechariah turned around and walked through the front door straight into the woods.

***

"Put it down! I said put it down!" Wyatt screamed. Somewhere in the distance, a door opened, and he heard the shuffling of feet. His body shook uncontrollably, and a warm wetness trickled down his pajama leg. He wrapped his arms around his chest, trying to shield himself from the crisp night air.

"Wyatt! What in the world are you doing out here?" Benji asked, grabbing him into his arms. "Are you okay? Are you hurt?" Miguel and Gideon were just behind him. Questions were thrown at Wyatt, but he didn't speak.

He looked back at the small garden as he was carried into the house and said, "Zechariah."

Chapter 18

"And now the whole town is nervous! I mean, the guy was nobody's favorite, but three people going missing in a short period? It gets people talking." Tammy, the grocery store cashier, was talking Miguel's ear off. Miguel, being a fan of local drama, did not mind at all.

"So, this new one was an abuser, right? Sounds like karma."

"Oh yeah, poor Kate used to come into this store with a shiner or two depending on how things at home were going." Tammy leaned forward and whispered, "Honestly, I can't help but think maybe this time she may have done him in and blamed the woods."

Miguel looked at Benji with concern before adding, "But this is happening a little TOO often, right? The police should be looking into this a bit more now, right?"

"Oh, the cops here are just as lazy as the politicians. Nothing out of the normal ever happens around here, so I wouldn't count on them any."

"The politicians are maybe a little more active than you may give them credit for, Tammy," the Mayor said as she walked in, interrupting them. "Maybe you should think a little more about what you say unless you want me to give your mom a call again."

"I didn't mean anything by it, Mayor Spruce! I'm just repeating what I heard, is all." She quickly shuffled the brown paper bags together and handed them to Benji, "Here you two go; thanks so much for coming." Tammy promptly walked away from the counter and started sweeping.

Outside the store, Miguel stood looking around at the townfolks going about their day. Nothing rushed them along. It was nothing like life in New York.

"Benji, I don't feel right."

"What's wrong, Peanut? You need to eat?"

"No, I'm talking about this town; it freaks me out." He looked around, "Something just always feels off around here."

Benji readjusted the bags he was carrying and looked at his watch. "I think you're still just adjusting."

"I don't know if I want to live here if people are disappearing. This is not a case of culture shock or being homesick. I really worry we might be in danger."

"Danger? Kind of extreme, don't you think? People get lost in the woods all the time, and these people are probably so bored they can't help but make up stories to entertain themselves. Yesterday at the clinic, I had a patient come in saying she thought her cat might have been possessed by her grandad. The other day, a couple had me check the vitals of their baby over and over again because they had heard stories about a changeling."

"Changeling?"

"Little creatures that replace babies. Fairies take the real babies to, I don't know, fairyland, I guess."

"Oh, wow." Miguel felt calmed by Benji's words until Mayor Spruce walked out of the store behind them. She had a bag filled with roots and plants and another with herbs sticking out the top.

"Making a witches brew at home?" Benji asked Spruce with a grin.

"Witches? Oh, they don't get anywhere close to what I'm doing, doctor," Spruce replied.

Miguel was shocked to hear what sounded like a joke come out of the stern old woman's mouth. However, she said it so dryly one could be forgiven for thinking she was sincere.

"You two take care now up in that dreary mansion. Let me know if you ever become interested in giving it to the town and making it an official landmark." She did not wait for a reply and briskly walked away up the road. Miguel wanted to run after her and take her up on that offer immediately. He just couldn't understand why.

"Still, I am worried about people disappearing in these woods. Maybe we need to talk to the kids about avoiding them from now on," he said to Benji.

"Well, yeah, I'm fine with that."

"Or we could take the mayor up on her offer and move back to the city?" Miguel said quickly and grinned, trying to seem half serious.

"I'm just establishing my practice, and we have a ton of repairs being done to the manor. The town can't afford to pay the debt that it is taking to restore that place."

Miguel looked away and noticed a missing poster for the old store owner and a more worn-down one for the town drunk. He couldn't help but mutter, "This is truly terrible."

Chapter 19

"This is truly Amazing!" Emma shouted at Channing in the hallway of their school.

"I don't know, Emma, you sure it's all connected?" Channing said in a whisper.

"Channing, three people are missing, and the woods were the last place they were seen. It's gotta be connected. Any decent detective would be able to see that. We should go back."

"Back? Did you forget what happened last time?"

"Good point."

"And what does it matter? We can't do a better job than the police," said Channing.

Emma furrowed her brow and felt upset at such an accusation. Why couldn't they do better than the police? The police seemed to be happy with calling every incident an accident. There had to be a reason behind that, and she knew it. "Hey, let's get out of here," she said.

"We still have a few minutes before class starts, though."

"No, I mean, let's get out of here," she said, wiggling her eyebrows and gesturing to the front doors of the school.

Emma could see that Changing was realizing what she meant when she saw his face turn white and his eyes widened, "Oh no. No no, no, no, no, no, nope. Can't do that." He lowered his voice further as he got closer to Emma, "Can't leave school. That would get us in serious trouble!"

Emma smiled and grabbed Channing's hand, interlocking their fingers and looking directly into his eyes, "You decided to be best friends with trouble." Channing blushed and tried to get out the words, best friend, but was suddenly pulled by Emma, who had his hand.

She made a full sprint toward the door without looking back to see if her friend was okay. When they reached the door, they pushed hard and swung them outward as the sunlight shined in. The moment the two of them were outside, they did not stop for anything, ducking behind cars and bushes as they made their way toward the town square. Emma had one target in mind: The Green Hollow public library. She feared what sort of heavy security they might encounter when they got there but figured they would be able to devise a battle plan if needed.

It didn't take long before she spotted the small brick building. It was rather tiny, in her opinion, but kept cleaner than the libraries she was used to back home. There were no spray-painted figures or swear words written on it, and just outside the doors were small red and yellow flowers. She wouldn't be fooled by the town's nice exterior, not when it had so many secrets.

Emma walked into the place, carefully observing her surroundings. She didn't see a guard force or even one serious security system in place. In fact, the library was completely empty except for an old lady who was busy shuffling some books around behind the front desk. Emma grabbed hold of Channing's hand and pulled him inside.

"So, what exactly are we looking for again?" Channing asked

"Town history stuff." She looked around, seeing only bookshelves. "I figured getting in would be the hard part. I really have no idea what I'm looking for."

"Well, that's great. So, we risk detention or worse just to realize we're still just kids?"

Emma thought for a moment and then decided on a risky idea. She turned to Channing and gave him a smile, which he had to now be aware meant she was about to do something dangerous, and walked back to the front counter. Emma couldn't see over the counter, even on her tippy toes, so she went over to the side where there was an opening. The older lady was still distracted by her work.

COUGH. Hggg. Emma cleared her throat.

"Did you just cough?" Channing asked.

It had the desired effect because the librarian turned to see them. She set down a book and moved slowly and carefully over to them. A moment passed until, finally, the older woman spoke, "Now, what are two sweet kids doing out of school?"

Emma saw her friend already start to buckle as the simple question made him look sweatier and shakier. She thought fast and replied, "We're homeschooled, ma'am." She looked at Channing, who, in turn, nodded his head. "Our parents sent us here to learn more about the history of our town. Could you help us with that?"

Another moment passed with Channing looking as though he wanted to cry until a big smile crept onto the lady's wrinkled face, "I would love to help you two! You remind me so much of my sister; she works in the city, or she did until she got old like me, ha-ha. Well, anyway, come with me, and I will take you to the town history section."

The kids went to move out of her way but realized she was still standing there. Once she began moving, she looked slow and cumbersome. Eventually, they made their way to a small clearing in the forest of books, where a single table sat. The librarian pointed to a couple of seats, and Emma sat down with Channing. When the Librarian was out of earshot, they started whispering to each other.

"She is going to call the school," said Channing.

"No, she isn't; she is probably getting us a laptop with all the info or maybe a video."

"Are you sure she believed we are homeschooled? Why would our parents let us come here alone?"

"Keep it down; it worked just fine. In a minute, we will have all the info we need."

Emma's excitement quickly changed to fear as she watched the older woman carrying what looked like a giant stack of old papers with a small book on top. When the stuff was dropped in front of them, Emma could hardly believe the table could manage the weight of it all.

"Um, ma'am?"

"Yes, dear?"

"You wouldn't happen to have this on any kind of device, would you?"

"Well, we did get a computer installed a while back."

"Oh, great!"

"But its been broken for about nine years now."

"Oh, great." Emma turned back to the stack of paper in front of her and let out a sigh. She looked over to Channing, who had already begun pulling documents off of the pile. Emma grabbed the small book, *A History of Green Hollow*, and decided against running back to school. She started slowly reading the first page. Emma put the book down proudly after finishing three pages. It was the oldest, driest, worst book she had ever read. She looked over to Channing only to find that half of the stack was moved over to his right, and he was reading faster than an Olympic sprinter runs.

"Channing?"

He looked up, almost as if coming out of a trance. "Hmm? Yes?"

"Did you read all those old papers?"

"Um, yes," he said, looking slightly embarrassed, "I, uh, like reading."

"Well, what did we learn?"

Channing shuffled through papers, looking around. He took a deep breath and said, "This town has been around since the late 1800s but only started printing its own newspaper in the early 1950s. So, there really isn't a whole lot to go off of here." Channing grabbed a specific newspaper and raised it up for Emma to see. "Except here, in the mid-60s, there were similar disappearances in the woods. At the time, people were worried it was some sort of serial killer, like the Zodiac or something."

"Whats a Zodiac?"

"Something my mom is really into, I think," he replied before continuing, "Anyway, after that, I started looking for similar stories, but they stopped after five disappearances."

"So, no one found out what happened?"

"Yeah, it sort of died down. The next news article just talks about a local pageant or something."

"Well, that doesn't tell us much."

"It might, actually." Channing shuffled Through more papers until producing a different newspaper, "This one's from the late 80s."

Emma's eyes were drawn to the title in bold: **DISAPPEARANCE IN WOODS.**

"Wait, what? Channing, you're a mad genius." Emma stood up and tried her best to make out the small font. "What does it say?"

"It's very similar to the one from the 60s. There had been three missing persons when it was written."

"So that means it might be happening again and again?"

"Every twenty years, give or take." Channing shook his head.

For a moment, Emma froze. Something felt off, and she did not feel they were alone like something had been listening in on them, "I think we should leave," she said. Channing looked at Emma and nodded his head in agreement. The two got up quietly and made their way toward the main entrance. The old librarian was not at her station.

"Let's head back now," Emma whispered.

They reached the doors and pushed and pulled but were unable to pry them open. "We're locked in!" Channing said. Emma desperately tried again, but the doors would not budge.

"We need to find another door," she said. They moved back through the library to find another door. They walked past the table they had used, but all the materials had been cleared away. Emma figured the librarian had put them away. She turned around to see if the librarian was at her desk, and when she did, she noticed a row of lights turning off in the distance. A chill ran down her spine as she watched row after row of lights clicking off until they were in darkness. Almost instantly, she felt as though someone or something was watching them.

"What's happening?" Emma whispered.

"I don't know, but I want to get out of here," Channing replied.

They stood there for a moment until her eyes adjusted. "There. I can see the bookcases. Follow me." They made their way along the aisles that were once straightforward but now twisted and turned like they were in a maze. She took a sharp right down a passage that appeared shorter than the rest. Emma looked back, checking on Channing, who was breathing heavily. When she looked forward again, the aisle had stretched until she could no longer see the end. They took another sharp right only to appear back at the table where they had researched the disappearances.

"We're going in circles!"

"I know, Channing. I know!"

"I think I'm having a panic attack," he said, breathing quickly.

Emma grabbed him by the shoulders, "We are going to get out of here! This is just a library; calm down." She let go of Channing and looked around, choosing a new path to take. They stopped at an intersection.

"I should have thrown a chair through the freaking front door," Emma said.

"How are we this lost? Channing screamed.

The whole place seemed to shift and change with every attempt to leave. Emma tossed her hands up to the back of her head and tried to think of something.

"We need to find an emergency exit." The moment Emma said it, a sign lit up in one of the aisles that read EXIT in green. Channing sprinted toward it while Emma cautiously followed. They both slammed into the door that gave way to bright daylight. For a moment, she exhaled a sigh of relief after feeling as though they might have somehow been trapped there forever. When her eyes adjusted, and they both looked up, any relief they had felt left when they saw what appeared to be a very formally dressed old woman next to the nice librarian. Her eyes shot like daggers and made Emma want to look away, but she was too stubborn to do so.

"You know, when I was in school, they used to bind our hands and drag us back if we were caught playing truant. Once we arrived there, they would beat us with a paddle for every hour we had missed." The formal old woman said as she looked at Emma and Channing, "Though I guess we could take you back in my car instead of tying you with rope."

"I am so sorry, Mayor Spruce, I truly didn't realize. The little one there reminded me so much of my sister, who you know moved up to the city to work until she became too old and..."

"It is quite alright, Dorian. I will handle it from here." Mayor Spruce walked over and knelt down in front of the two of them, "Now, I hope what you two discovered in there was worth the trouble you are in now," she said with a wicked smile.

Chapter 20

Gideon lay on his bed late at night, looking at the black and white photo of the man and woman. After finding it in Wyatt's closet, it had taken up a lot of space in his head as he thought about it. He wondered who they were and why they had come to this house. Why did the woman dressed so elegantly in white seem so sad? He wasn't even sure how he knew she was sad, but the more he looked at it, the more it seemed to speak to him. He also couldn't help but think that the woman's hair was a beautiful dark color, something he admired about Agatha as well. Eventually, after recognizing the time, he put the picture down and sat up, rubbing his eyes.

"What is wrong with me?" Gideon said aloud. He had spent so much time staring at the stupid picture that he hadn't thought about his important game tomorrow, "Not very smart, Gideon," he said to himself. He looked up from his hand and heard the sound of floorboards creaking. For a moment, Gideon held his breath and stayed as still as possible. *Creak.* The sound of the old wood confirmed his suspicions, and he bolted up to his feet, walked carefully to his door, and slowly opened it. When the crack was big enough for his right eye to see, he instantly calmed down.

"Wyatt, go back to sleep, kid!" Gideon yelled out from his doorway. When Wyatt seemed to have ignored him, Gideon swung his door open and stepped out into the hallway, "Wyatt! What's the matter with you?" With no answer again, Gideon thought about rushing over and grabbing Wyatt but decided against it and walked behind his brother to see where it would lead. He was amazed at how careful a sleepwalking kid could be moving down those giant stairs. Wyatt wobbled as he walked without the support of his brace. Gideon watched as he leaped up to grab the door handle and push it open. The cold air made him shiver, yet Wyatt stayed stiff, walking robotically toward his goal. Wyatt stepped into the garden and stood for a long period in front of the statue of the woman. Gideon walked briskly toward it and decided to try and move his brother. Wyatt was cold to the touch, and even though his eyes were closed and he was supposedly sleeping, he fought off his brother's attempts to move him. Gideon, frustrated, decided to pick him up altogether.

"Get off me! Get off me! I won't let you bury me again!" Wyatt screamed in a voice that only faintly sounded like his own. Gideon dropped him on the ground, and Wyatt scrambled to get up and return to his position facing the statue.

"Wyatt, You are really freaking me out here, kid, what is happening to you? Why are you doing this?"

Wyatt turned his head to the side and uttered, "To show you." Then he dropped to the ground and rolled into a fetal position. Gideon walked up to his brother and casually checked to see if he was still asleep. He lifted Wyatt up to take him back in, and as he turned around, his eyes widened, and his skin went pale. Gideon almost dropped his brother for a second time. He took a step backward and ended up hitting his head on the statue behind him. The pain was sharp and made him want to scream out, but he didn't let himself as fear had set in, and his fight or flight response could not decide what to do about the tall, pale woman in all white standing at the woodline. She was perfectly still, seemingly fixed on Gideon's location. Gideon only looked away once to check how far he would have to run to get back inside.

When he returned his gaze to the woman, his panic only hastened as she appeared to have moved to the middle of the open field between the house and the woods in the blink of an eye. The distance to his door suddenly felt like miles. He looked down at Wyatt and decided he had to try and sprinted to the front of the house, keeping his eyes on the white figure. The woman seemed to not move this time, but as he made it to the door, he looked back. To his horror, the pale woman was standing in front of the statue. She seemed to be completely ignoring him and his brother. She just stared at the statue in the garden that Wyatt had been found sleeping under night after night.

Gideon kept his eyes on the large creature but slowly moved his hand to open the door. He couldn't help but notice her alien-like features. Still possibly recognizable as a woman, she had long fingers with sharp fingernails and long black hair that covered her face. She was almost as tall as the statue she was fixated on. Gideon grabbed the handle, heard a faint click of the door, and carefully pulled it open. The creature broke her gaze and slowly turned her head to face him. Her red eyes pierced his, and he felt himself frozen in fear. Gideon, breaking his gaze, rushed into the manor and slammed the door shut behind him.

He locked the door with trembling fingers as quickly as he could manage. He paused for a moment to catch his breath, still holding his brother. What was he supposed to do now? It didn't take long before he realized he had to call the police. He ran to the front parlor with Wyatt and laid him gingerly on the couch before grabbing the phone next to him on a small end table. He dialed the number and waited. His heart quickened with each unanswered ring. *Come on*, he begged in his head.

"Hello"

***

"I was with you until you said this woman was the size of a statue… hold on." Outside the manor, the sheriff pulled a flashlight from his belt and shined the light at Gideon's.

Gideon winced and placed his arm over his eyes.

"Just a moment. I'm a doctor; I think I'd know if my nephew was on drugs," Benji said, stepping between Gideon and the sheriff. The sheriff was a muscular man, not very tall, but thick with blue tattoos that were visible beneath his rolled sleeves. He had short black hair, a handlebar mustache, and a scar under his left eye. Gideon got the impression he wasn't a man to fire warning shots. "The bottom line is that my nephew saw a crazy woman running around our back yard. I think you should have a look around."

"Plan on it. I'm just making sure I get the story straight, is all." As the Sheriff scribbled some notes into his pad, the sound of Mayor Spruce's car pulling up made all of them turn to look. Spruce got out of the car, made her way up to the group, and instantly took charge. She gave the Sheriff a nod and then gave Miguel and Benji a curious look as they both stood there in matching robes. She turned back to the officer. "Sheriff Colin, why don't you take a walk around the perimeter and make sure everything is secure so these nice folks can go back to bed?" Colin looked back at the family and then nodded in agreement and turned, grumbling something incoherent as he walked off with his flashlight at the ready. When he turned the corner and was no longer visible, the Mayor turned back to the family. "It's been quite an active last couple of days, hasn't it?"

"Is it common for the mayor to make appearances at routine police calls, or is this somehow a special circumstance?" Miguel remarked.

"Oh, now, what sort of civil servant would I be if I didn't check on the newest addition to our town every once in a while."

"Feels like we've seen a lot of you recently," Benji added.

"Small towns have a habit of making things feel that way, don't they?" Gideon felt that Spruce knew it made no sense that she had come out here tonight and didn't care. She answered vaguely, and her eyes had a habit of looking past them at the house as if something kept calling to her.

"Mayor Spruce." Gideon cleared his throat. "How much do you know about this house?"

She looked at Gideon inquisitively. "I know this place has been a thorn in my side for a long time."

"How so?" Gideon asked.

"I have a large patch of land with a hideous manor house that does little to benefit this town. I could have developed this land into something beneficial, but your family had an ironclad hold on the property."

"I'm sorry our home is such a problem for you," Miguel replied.

"No problem at all." As she had said that, Sheriff Colin appeared on the other side of the manor.

"Nothing out of the ordinary here, ma'am."

"Well then, that's settled. Have yourself a lovely night." Mayor Spruce didn't wait for anyone to return her goodbyes and drove off with the Sheriff following behind. Benji and Miguel walked into the manor first. Gideon watched the cars until they were out of site and then turned to face the statue. His mind raced with what he had seen, and he tried to figure out how he could convince them it happened. Of course, what he really wished he could understand was why any of this was happening at all.

Chapter 21

"I love my husband, but he is dumber than rocks," Brandy-Sue said after a long swig of her spiked coffee.

"Be nice to your man, Brandy. I'm sure he tries his best," Miguel replied. Having already downed a cup of coffee, he was feeling a lot more comfortable. The two were enjoying brunch outside on the porch. It started with normal coffee before Brandy-Sue revealed a small bottle of whiskey. Miguel was happy to have finished decorating the house. When he was in town, he had found a nice patio set that made the porch more cozy. Miguel had been so stressed out with all the weird things happening in the house that he was at ease listening to his friend Brandy-Sue complain about her husband and gossip about the town.

"I swear some days I feel like I need to move out of this one-horse town," she said, taking another big gulp of her drink, "It feels like everyone here is comfortable living boring, mundane lives." Miguel laughed because he knew she didn't mean it. She loved this town and all its quirks, but when she got to drinking, she not only insulted the town but her husband too, despite loving both dearly. He had come to realize that she wasn't so bad to be around once you got used to her. "The worst of them is that Mayor Spruce! How she got to be an elected official here is beyond me. I mean, how long has she been the mayor?"

"Yeah, she made it clear she didn't like us here in this manor last night. Just an intense woman, really," Miguel said, pouring himself a virgin coffee.

At that, Brandy's eyes suddenly narrowed like a hawk honing in on its prey. "Wait a minute. Why was the mayor at your place last night?"

"Oh, Gideon, I guess. He saw some crazy lady in white running around the front yard."

"Okay, wait. I need the full story." Brandy poured herself a non-virgin coffee and began absorbing every detail that Miguel remembered from that night. "And why would Spruce need to be here for all that? Why was she even called?"

"Oh, I have no idea; she acted kind of weird about it all."

CRASH.

Both Miguel and Brandy sue stood up with an urgency that only parents do when hearing a loud noise. They rushed into the house to see where the noise came from

"Wyatt!" Miguel yelled.

No answer. They listened in silence, hoping that Wyatt would reveal himself. However, the only sound they heard came from the room where Emory stayed on the bottom floor. He was talking to himself, which was not unusual, but one word was seemingly being repeated.

"Dirt." It started as a whisper and progressively got louder. " Dirt, dirt, dirt." Emory's voice of Emory was clear as Brandy-Sue and Miguel walked into his room. Emory had his back to them.

"I just want it; I need it," he kept saying to himself, giggling. He seemed animated.

"What do you mean, Emory?" Miguel asked.

Emory's head twisted around in his wheelchair, and with a big smile said, "You all beneath the dirt!"

The sound of Wyatt screaming entered the room, and Miguel, with no time to process what had happened, sprinted to meet it. The screaming continued while Miguel went from room to room, desperately looking for Wyatt until he reached the entrance to the basement. The screaming stopped, but Miguel knew it had to have come from there. He looked down the staircase and saw Wyatt standing with his back facing him.

"Wyatt, are you okay?" Miguel asked, walking slowly toward the entrance. Before he could take his first step down the stairs, however, the door slammed closed in his face. The pain of the hardwood hitting his nose sent waves of pain through his face. He hunched over, holding his nose and cursing bilingually as blood began to pour out of his nostrils. He ignored the pain and the blood and ran at the door, slamming his shoulder into it and screaming, "Wyatt, open the door!" Miguel ignored the blood all over his shirt and smeared it into the door as he rammed into it once more, "Please, please open the door, Wyatt!"

"Miguel, let's try together, okay?" Brandy-Sue said, grabbing Miguel's shoulder. They rammed into the door at the same, feeling a slight give in the frame. They both reeled back, and with one more solid hit, the door swung open, and the wooden frame splintered into pieces. Miguel tripped on the stairs and fell to his side on the hard floor. He looked up to see Wyatt's back still facing him and what looked like the figure of a grown man in a petty coat and top hat standing in front of him. Miguel lifted his arm.

"Get away from him!" he shouted, lifting himself up despite the tremendous pain in his shoulder, but when he got back on his feet, the figure was gone. Miguel ran over to Wyatt and held him tight.

"What just happened?" Brandy-Sue asked, walking carefully over to him.

Miguel turned to her, releasing Wyatt. "I have no idea what is happening around here! None! It's one thing after another with this house. Strange sounds, thinking kids are in a room when they aren't, some crazy lady running around our yard, and now I'm seeing people who aren't there."

"Okay, okay." She knelt down to Wyatt's eye level. "Why don't you go play in your room for a little." Wyatt nodded and ran past her up the stairs out of sight.

"Are you saying that this house is haunted?" She raised an eyebrow and leaned in closer as if someone might hear them.

"I don't know, I don't know what I'm saying." Miguel raised his arms in defeat. "You have an explanation for this?"

"Oh, my goodness. The same thing happened to a distant cousin of mine," she said.

Miguel sighed. "Oh. Great."

Chapter 22

Gideon ran to the side of the field, where there were tables set up, to grab some water after his drills. Ricky and Daniel followed behind him. "You know, you're good. No one doubts that, but you play like you're the only guy out there. That might be fine for city hockey, but down here, it takes more than a few fancy hat tricks to be part of the team."

Gideon was already annoyed. "To be honest, I never really notice any of you on the field. Ill have to keep my eyes open during the next game."

Daniel scrunched up his face, and it began to go red, but Ricky grinned, clearly getting the joke. "That's funny, man; maybe use it in your next stand-up routine. You'd be good there, standing all alone in a spotlight." Daniel and Ricky shared a laugh that Daniel could tell made Gideon more upset.

"Yeah, well anyway, what's the deal about you seeing some crazy lady at your house last night? Was that your mom or something?"

"My mom's dead," Gideon said, knowing how quickly that would suck the air out of Daniel's sails. Gideon noticed Agatha approaching out of the corner of his eye. He turned away from his fellow teammates, but not before catching Ricky punching Daniel's arm.

"Hey," Gideon said, turning to Agatha. He got a waft of her perfume. It was mild and a bit fruity.

"Can I talk to you real quick?" She asked, motioning toward the corner of the building where no one was standing.

"Sure." Gideon followed her to the more secluded area. He had no idea what she would say, but his heart sped up just a bit. "What's up?"

Agatha tucked a strand of her dark hair behind her ear and dug through her large purse. "Okay, so I know it might seem odd, but I did some research into your house," she started to say while pulling out a few pieces of paper. "I found a copy of that picture you had."

Gideon grabbed the photo, seeing the familiar man and woman. The second picture was of the house, and there was some writing on the bottom.

"It turns out that it's the founder and his wife. She is your great, great, great grandmother... or something like that."

"That's interesting," Gideon replied. He couldn't get why that was important enough to come all the way to the field to tell him.

"You realize how important your ancestors are to this town, right?"

"I know that he founded this place way back then. Not much else, though."

"Every child here is brought up learning the myth of how the town was created."

"Oh, another history lesson then?"

"Shut up, listen; the story goes that your ancestor rode on giants, smashing down the trees and creating the spot the town is built on. This town was built as a safe refuge for Irish immigrants who were being persecuted during his time, your great grandfather being an immigrant himself."

"Giants? I wonder how they got them on the boats," said Gideon. Agatha laughed, which made Gideon proud.

"Seriously, shut up. The giants helped to found the town, and then all matter of mythical folk appeared and helped build things to his specifications. It all went as planned, and the people were safe, but the founder held a dark secret that would cost him everything."

"It's a cute story, but what does it have to do with me?"

"Well, his wife disappeared, and no one knows what happened to her. Our town's founder supposedly drank himself to death in your old cellar."

"Creepy," Miles added.

Surprised, they both turned to see Miles.

"Dude, you have a crazy woman running through your yard, and now this?"

"How does everybody know about that already?" Gideon replied

"What if that isn't just a crazy woman, though?" Agatha added

"You know, too? Seriously, is there a gossip hotline in this town?" Gideon described all the details of what had happened, including the surprise visit from the mayor. Miles looked excited, but Agatha was focused, seemingly analyzing every detail of the story.

"It was all pretty strange, but honestly, it was dark, and I was worried about my brother."

Agatha moved closer to Gideon and grabbed his hand, "I believe you saw something more than just a woman dressed in all white. This town is filled with strange happenings that go beyond what we can comprehend." She seemed sad as she said it, almost as if the thought brought painful memories. "Well, maybe we ought to take another look around that manor of yours." Miles put his arms around Gideon and Agatha.

Gideon shrugged Miles off. "Yeah, sure, we can do some more exploring if you want to. Let me just tell the coach I have to take off." He ran off to tell the coach he needed to head home for something important. Then, the three of them got into Agatha's car to head to the manor. Miles pulled a cassette out of his pocket, put it into the tape deck, and before anyone was ready, a loud and strange sound that could possibly be defined as music started blasting out of the speakers at high volume. Gideon gave Miles an annoyed look, but his friend was oblivious as he began to dance vigorously.

"I feel bad for the seatbelt," said Agatha.

Chapter 23

"Listen, you two, no funny business, okay?" Brandy-Sue said, looking down at Emma and Channing. "You two just need to play nice and keep your noses out of trouble. Do you understand?

"Yes, Mom."

"Yes, ma'am."

"Oh ha-ha, ma'am! Like, I'm some 80-year-old spinster! Well, anyway, I'm going to be in the manor helping Miguel out with some things. So again, STAY OUT OF TROUBLE!" With that said, she turned around and walked into the manor. The kids looked back and saw Mary on a bicycle riding in with a brown bag.

"Hey, children," she said, carefully removing her helmet and setting it on the seat.

"Hi, Miss Mary," Emma replied.

"Don't tell your brothers, but...." she pulled out a bag of candy from her groceries," You two enjoy." Channing looked at the colorful bag as if it was a sack of gold coins. After a chorus of thank yous, the kids ran off to the side of the house. Emma looked back to make sure they weren't being watched before pulling out a large spool of string. She tossed it up in the air, catching it as Channing looked at her with terror, knowing they were about to do something wrong again.

"What are you planning to do with that?"

"Oh, I just figured out a way we can explore more of the woods without getting lost again."

"Why can't we just do normal kid things?"

"Because normal kids are boring, that's why you hang out with me! Now come on, we are losing daylight here." They moved to the edge of the woodline, staring into the mass of trees. Emma took the first end of the string and tied it to a low-hanging branch. Once she was sure the knot was tight, she rolled the big spool out, motioning for Channing to follow.

"How did you get your hands on all this string?"

"Miguel bought it, thinking he was going to get into sewing. It was sat on a shelf with his other failed hobbies, including woodworking, stamp collecting, and even puppet making."

"Puppet making?"

"Yeah, my uncle is eccentric."

"Eccentric?"

"That's the one!" Emma and Channing slowly and carefully moved into the woods, eating candy and talking about random stuff to pass the time. Emma stopped every few trees to wind the string around one. They felt confident about the method and went deeper into the woods than they ever had before. Emma tried her best to look around at anything that seemed off or strange. Other than a few squirrels and a couple of loud birds, nothing out of the ordinary jumped out for them. After some time had passed, they sat down under a tree to take a short break.

"How far do you think we've gone?" Channing asked.

"Oh, I'm sure at least a hundred miles." Emma looked around. "Maybe two hundred." When she said that, something caught her ear that sounded out of place. At first, she couldn't tell if it was an animal or not. The sound came from the left of them. It was like a long, drawn-out moan.

"You hear that, right?" Emma asked.

"Yeah, that's a bird, right?" Channing replied.

"Maybe, maybe not. Let's go check it out." Emma stood up and began pulling her string toward where the moaning sound came from. Channing followed close behind. The closer they got, the more the sound resonated and sounded as if it was coming from something massive.

"Maybe we don't want to know what is making that sound, Emma!"

"Come on! Where's your sense of adventure?"

"About two hundred miles back." Emma looked up and noticed they were heading toward a clearing where light was able to penetrate the dense forest. They entered the clearing and were amazed to see giant rocks protruding from the ground.

"Woah! How did these get here?" Emma said.

"I have no idea," Changing replied. The clearing had five large stones, one of them at the center while the other four encircled it. They were both startled as a large black bird with white eyes sat perched on top of the middle stone with its beak ajar, croaking that unnatural, almost human-sounding moan. It looked down at Emma and twisted its neck to the side.

"Heeeeeeeeeere." The bird squawked, "Here!" It said again before flying away.

They looked at each other, and an uneasy feeling settled in the pit of Emma's stomach. She put the string down to examine the stones more closely.

"Hey, look, there are little swirly things on these rocks, too," Emma observed.

"They all seem to have them; I wish I knew what they meant," said Channing. Emma approached the center stone and raised her hand to touch the cool rock. Placing her fingers on it, she felt something pulsate. She felt a sudden jolt of energy. Channing walked up to her, concerned.

"Are you okay?"

"Yeah, yeah, it shocked me or something." In an instant, whispers entered Emma's mind, forcing her to her knees. Suddenly, she heard several loud voices screaming out in pain. It became so overwhelming that she closed her eyes and covered her ears with her hands. Her chest grew tighter and tighter until she felt as if there was a seatbelt across her body. Then came the sound of cars screeching around her. It engulfed her entire surroundings, and the last sounds of her parents, as they crashed the vehicle, echoed in her mind. Why did this keep happening to her? When she came to, it was beginning to get darker. Channing was sitting next to her.

"Emma!" He wiped tears from his eyes. "I was so scared."

For a moment, she didn't know where she was. Her eyes darted around her, but it was hard to focus on anything other than the pressure she felt over her whole body. She took a few uneasy breaths and soon remembered where they were. Emma got up and faked a smile, "It's okay, I'm okay," she said, wiping away tears from her eyes. She looked around until she spotted the spool she had left on the ground. Although it had rolled a bit, she found comfort in seeing it there. She turned back to Channing, who was looking at the stones.

"Those big rocks did something to me," she said.

"I saw that," Channing replied. "It's strange, but there's something familiar about them." He reached out a hand toward one of them.

"Channing, stop!" Emma yelled.

Channing instantly dropped his arm and turned around. "Sorry," he said. Then his eyes widened, and he pointed behind Emma, "The string, look!" Emma turned around and saw the spool was being pulled slightly away from them. It moved only a little, but it acted as if it was pulled from some unknown force. They looked at each other, and both began creeping closer to it as if they were afraid it would be scared off like a small animal. Then, as if it knew they were coming, the spool skipped away from them.

"Our string!" Channing yelled as they sprinted toward it. They grabbed on to either side of the spool, but the string unwound from it. They fell backward, still holding the empty spool.

"What's happening?" Channing screamed.

"I don't know," Emma said, trying to see where the detached string was now that it had flown off into the dark forest.

"No, please, no," Emma screamed, throwing the spool down, "This can't be happening. Why is this happening?" This time, tears formed and poured down her face. She had had enough and just wanted to be home. Before she realized what was happening, Channing grabbed her hand and began sprinting as fast as he could through the trees.

"C'mon, I think I can still hear it," Channing yelled back at her. They followed the sound of the string as it scraped on the trees. Emma looked at her usually cowardly friend with awe as he kept pace with the sound. Finally, they couldn't run anymore; their little legs were unable to push them at the rate they needed to go. They stood hunched over as more daylight disappeared.

"I really hope that got us close," Channing said in between pants.

"You did great. Now, let's hope another miracle happens." Emma hoped maybe the sparkling lights that had saved them before would come again. However, after a while of waiting, they knew that was unlikely. They sat in silence until a sound neither of them could have expected found its way to them in the darkness. It was something loud that both of them agreed could have been maybe called music but sounded more like the clanging of pans and a weird techno beat. They listened for where it was coming from and ran toward it with whatever strength they had left. Emma closed her eyes for a moment and hoped with everything she had that this would work. She gripped Channing's hand tightly.

"There!" Channing yelled, and they both charged through an opening in the woods that led to the small road up to the manor. Once out, they noticed that the strange sounds were coming from Agatha's car. Emma had never felt happier to see her older brother.

Chapter 24

"Emma!" For a moment, Gideon squinted to make sure it was really his sister and her pale friend walking up the road to them. They looked exhausted and half-wild as they approached him and his friends. Gideon and Agatha ran to them and knelt down, checking them all over for wounds. The kids were still catching their breath. Gideon noticed his sister's tear-stained cheeks. The last time he had seen her like that was at their parent's funeral.

"What happened to you two?" Agatha asked.

Channing attempted to speak, but his heart was still beating fast from running, and his words were interrupted by gulps of fresh air. "The woods, loud bird. The string was gone."

"Did any of that translate to English for you?" Gideon asked Agatha, who shrugged. Gideon walked his sister over to the porch. After a few minutes and a glass of water from the kitchen, Emma attempted to explain what had happened to them. They all sat on the porch and went back and forth, talking about the different and strange things going on in the town. Gideon brought up his encounter with the creature in their yard the other night and the photo that he couldn't stop thinking about. Emma went on to describe what had been happening in the woods the last few times they had gone there.

"And you went back in?" Gideon yelled. "What were you thinking?"

"She's young; either of us might have done the same at their age," said Miles.

"He's right," Agatha added while pulling a small bottle from her purse, "What we should be focusing on is how the mayor factors into all of this. She has been acting odd lately." Agatha shook the bottle and sprayed it around them, gaining odd looks from everyone. "What? It's lemongrass, cypress and rosemary! It cleanses negative energy."

"Right. I feel fully cleansed," said Gideon. As they spoke, the sun slowly sank behind the canopy of trees, bringing forth the night. Gideon stood up to turn on the porch light, and while doing so, he felt a shift happen in the atmosphere of the forest. It was like a living, breathing organism taking note of the day's end. After hearing what Emma had gone through in the copse, it was hard not to see the whole thing as cursed.

"So, we are spying on her?" Emma exclaimed, suddenly excited again.

Gideon shook his head sternly and pointed a finger at her. "*We* aren't doing anything. You're sitting this one out."

"No, I'm not! And if you try and make me, I'll tell Benji and Miguel everything."

The tension between the siblings was palpable. Both attempted to stand their ground until Gideon finally buckled with a loud, "Aghh, fine!" Gideon turned to his friends and took a long breathe, "We will have to tell Benji and Miguel something."

"What? Tell them we plan to follow and spy on a cranky elected official. That won't jive well with your folks?" Miles said

"Yeah, no, I think we are going to go to a movie together. That should work," said Gideon.

"They have a movie theater here?" asked Emma honestly.

Miles, Agatha, and Channing shared offended looks before Agatha replied in her best bumkin accent: "Well, normally we just watch butter churn all day until the one tractor is available to ride, but yeah, occasionally we allow ourselves to indulge in one of them moving picture shows."

"Yes, Emma, they got one of those here," Gideon replied.

"My mom is still here, too," Channing added.

"Right, so that works out pretty well then," Gideon said.

"We can't go into it with Miguel half-cocked, though. We need movie times, where it's at, and a phone number in case of emergencies." As they worked out the details, the family van pulled in, parked, and an exhausted Benji stepped out without looking up at any point as he made his way to the door.

Gideon looked around at everyone before saying, "Hey Benji, we're thinking about going to see a movie tonight."

Before Gideon could finish, Benji replied, "Okay, have fun."

Gideon, stunned at how little he had to bargain, decided to try for a little more. "Oh, also, can we barrow the van? We can't all fit in Agi's car."

Benji stopped and turned his head to look at Gideon. The dark bags under his eyes showed clearly. After a moment, he sighed. "Yeah, sure, just be safe out there." He tossed the keys to Gideon and walked into the house. The group took off to the van before the overworked uncle could have a change of heart. Once they were inside and Gideon had started the engine, he paused for a moment. "Uncle Benji seemed a little off tonight, don't you think?"

"Yeah, he must be doing like a thousand surgeries or something," Emma replied.

Gideon shook the weird feeling off and began driving away.

***

On the drive toward the town square, the group went back and forth on how to best find the mayor. Gideon was driving the van while Agatha sat in the front passenger seat. The rest sat in the back, Miles in the middle seat between Channing and Emma, despite there being a whole row of seats behind them. "What's the plan?" Miles asked.

"We have to figure out where the mayor is. So, I guess we should start at her office, then check her house. If she's not there, we will just have to go from place to place until we find her," Gideon replied.

"She's probably at the brewery," said Channing.

"How do you know that?" Gideon asked.

"Because my mom goes there a lot, and the mayor is there most nights."

Gideon deflated in his seat and then replied, "Okay, yeah, I guess we'll start there."

The van pulled up in front of the town brewery. It seemed to be a busy night with a good amount of the townspeople relaxing after a long week. Gideon noticed that a tall man stood guard in front of the place, letting people in. Agatha seemed to see that, too.

"Pull up to the side and then park. We have to get past security, and I have an idea for that," said Agatha. Gideon did as she said and parked to the left of the building. There was no one there, just a few trash cans and a small door. After he parked, he turned around to talk to everyone.

"Okay, Agi, Miles, and I are going to go in there to see what we can find. Emma, you and your friend just stay here and watch the van."

"Bull!" Emma shouted

"Don't argue with me. It's not safe in there, and you two stick out like a sore thumb."

"You guys suck! You're keeping your best player off the ice."

"It's not happening, okay?" As Gideon spoke, Emma crossed her arms and looked out the window. Channing seemed perfectly content to sit there. The three teens got out of the van and walked toward the side door of the brewery, attempting to be as quite as possible.

"This is child endangerment!" screamed Emma from the window of the passenger seat. Gideon looked back at her, narrowing his eyes, and promptly sped up to reach the door.

"I see staff smoking out here all the time. They prop the door open with a brick so they don't get locked out," Agatha stated as they came up to the door. Just as she had said, the door was held open by a small red brick next to an old can filled with cigarette buds. Once inside, Gideon turned around and kicked the brick, causing the door to shut and lock.

"Why did you do that?" asked Miles.

"Because my sister doesn't listen."

The three of them made it into the bar room, which was crowded and packed by what seemed like half the town. It felt weird to Gideon because it was a weeknight. It was hard to see past all the different faces surrounding them, so they did their best to weave through the crowd. Gideon saw that Agatha was close behind him but couldn't spot Miles anywhere until he looked toward the bar and saw him attempting to wave at the bartender for a drink. He shook his head and continued his search, figuring Miles would get easily distracted anyway. Scanning the walls, Gideon spotted the mayor near the back, walking ahead of a jolly-looking guy in suspenders who, for a moment, looked as if he was looking over at them. The guy in suspenders winked, and suddenly, the place seemed to swell with music and dancing. Gideon pressed forward to catch up and looked back at Agatha, who he thought was still following close behind, but was surprised to see she was swept up in dancing with random people.

"Agatha, what are you doing?"

"I'm sorry. It seemed rude not to join in," Agatha yelled back as she spun back and forth with different partners.

Gideon, visibly confused, looked over to Miles, who was downing a giant mug of something amber in the bar area. His friends had lost their minds in here. He shook it off and pressed on alone, walking into a hallway in the back past some restrooms before noticing the light of an open office door in the back. He crept up next to the open door and listened in to the mayor talking to the big ginger man.

"It's different this time because the bloodline has returned, Leath. There is no room for errors," the mayor said.

"You need to relax and learn to let your hair down a bit. You're still so young and passionate."

Spruce looked at him. "The signs are pointing to a new victim."

"Oh yeah? What poor unfortunate person has found themself on the chopping block this time?"

"I don't pick the victims," she said dryly. "We need to be more vigilant this time. The winds are shifting, and I don't like it."

"Well, I am forever at your service, of course." He laughed as he said it.

"Once again, you turn everything into a joke. Just be ready for whatever the manor tries to do next. That family is unlikely to be equipped to deal with this."

Gideon attempted to lean in closer, hoping to hear more of what they were saying. In doing so, he accidentally pulled a frame off the wall, causing it to crash on the floor. The mayor and her companion fell silent. Gideon panicked and made his way back to the bar room, but as he entered, a grizzly sight lay before him. The once cheerful music was missing notes and screeching as the violin played on. All the dancers were barefoot, with blood staining the bottom of their feet. Sweat and tears drizzled down their faces and bodies. Agatha looked like she had aged thirty years as she continued to sway to the music. Miles sat at the bar, still pouring pint after pint into his mouth. He was bloated by all the drink, and he couldn't keep anything in anymore, choking as it simply ran back out of his mouth. Gideon could do nothing but stare, frozen in place, until a voice came from right next to him.

"Such curious young minds sneaking into a man's brewery just to eavesdrop on a private conversation." Gideon whipped his head to the right to see Leath leaning on the wall next to him. "The funny thing is, I felt you in this place the moment you kicked that brick out the door, Gideon Kavanagh." Leath stood up straight and crossed his arms, smiling. "Don't get me wrong, I am in no way cross with you and your friends. I just thought I'd have a little fun, is all."

"You call this nightmare fun?" Gideon pointed toward the bar, and as both he and Leath turned to look, everything seemed to return to normal. The music was fun and light again, and everyone was dancing with Miles at the bar, clapping to it all, "I don't under..."

"Stand? You don't understand a lot yet, my boy. Such a heavy burden does that family of yours lay on your shoulders." He put his large hand on Gideon's shoulder, "Listen, lad, you and your friends take off now; I've had my fun." He leaned in. "Remember, though, that manor casts a darker shadow than any giant over this town." Leath straightened back up. "Oh, also, go get your sister and her little friend from the kitchen before she makes an even bigger mess. I'd hate for Mayor Spruce to turn you all in by informing your parents." At that, Gideon ran into the bar room, grabbing Agatha's hand and motioning Miles to go toward the kitchen.

"What's wrong? Did you find the mayor?

"Yeah, yeah, that and more. But we have to go now. I'll tell you more in the van." They all made their way through the dancing, drunken patrons and reached the kitchen, where Emma stood in the middle, caked in food with a skillet in one hand and a roller in another.

"Emma, why?"

"Well, the door you guys went through was locked, so we had to find another way in. I spotted this window, so I got Channing to lift me up to it, but he is pretty strong for his age, so I ended up going right through the dang thing. Then I was in this kitchen, and all these people in white coats were angry at me and yelling a lot."

"Okay, just put down the stuff and come with us."

Emma complied, and they all raced out the side door where Channing paced nervously by the van. They hopped into the vehicle, and after a moment, Gideon described everything he had heard and seen inside.

"Did that big guy spike your drink or something?" Miles asked.

"I didn't drink anything," Gideon replied

"Well, that makes two of us. The barman did not believe I had a growth hormone deficiency either."

"I don't know how he did it. It was like some sort of illusion or something. Honestly, it all seemed so real at the time."

The van fell silent for a while. No one was sure what to say. The first one to break the silence was Agatha, "Can you just help me understand what you heard the mayor say a little better?"

Gideon looked over at Agatha, "It sounded like she knew why people were disappearing, even who would be next. I wish I had heard her say who was next."

"Damn it!" Agatha yelled as she slammed her hands on the dash of the van, "Damn them all!"

Woah! You alright, Agi?" Miles asked. She sat there staring out into the distance for a while as she regained her composure.

"What's going on? Gideon asked.

"I'm sorry. Listen, I've seen this before, and I think we can stop this." Agatha looked over at Gideon, "We have to stop this."

"She's right, let's do it!" Emma chimed in from the back, still caked with flour and food.

"Woah, wait a minute, guys. We still have no idea what is happening and who is next!" Miles said.

Gideon looked into Agatha's eyes and saw how sad she was behind the anger. "Well, we know someone has been chosen, so we just need a way to scope out who that might be. Agatha, you said you know some way to do that?" he asked gingerly.

"Yes, The people act strange, like a zombie, toward the end. They start hearing and seeing things. They also begin to zone out a lot."

"That isn't going to be easy to spot," Channing replied.

"Well, there is another thing." Agatha shifted in her seat. "The person, well, I think maybe magpies are connected."

"What kind of pies?" Gideon asked.

"No, sorry, crows. I think they tend to be around them as they become strange."

Gideon wondered how she came upon all this info but shook it off. "Okay, so, then, now, we need a way to spot all these signs."

"The festival," Emma shouted. "I'm sure the whole town is going to be there."

"So we find this person and follow him. If it is supposed to happen soon, then it shouldn't take long," said Agatha.

"Whoever it is will freak if they think we are stalking them," Miles said

"Well, we are stalking. We're stalking them for the greater good," Agatha replied.

Everyone seemed a bit uneasy, but Agatha stood firm. "This can work, guys. The festival is this weekend, so I am going to be there looking for them."

"Woah, wait. You can't do that alone! People are disappearing," Gideon said

"Well, I did expect you to come with me," Agatha replied.

Gideon's face felt suddenly warm, and he cleared his throat. "Well, yeah, we're all friends, aren't we?" He looked forward out the front window. "Okay, so, I guess that's the plan. I'll take everyone back home, and we will meet back up this weekend.

Chapter 25

Miguel closed the bedroom door behind him. He heard the sound of running water and knew Benji was in the bathroom. The room was dark except for a sliver of light escaping the bathroom from beneath the door. A chill ran through Miguel, and he rubbed his arms, glancing from one corner of the room to another. Deciding to check the room before Benji was finished, he rushed to flip on the lights and knelt down, looking under the bed. Nothing. He quickly made his way to the closet. Besides hanging shirts and some random boxes left unpacked, there wasn't anything to take note of.

"What are you doing?" Benji asked. Miguel paused only a moment before continuing to check the rest of the room.

Without looking at Benji, Miguel replied, "I'm just checking some stuff."

"Some stuff?" Benji, who was halfway through brushing his teeth, shook his head and went back into the bathroom to spit. "What stuff?" he yelled from the bathroom.

"Just stuff, Benji!" Miguel looked behind the dresser and, when he felt satisfied with his work, turned to face Benji, who came back out of the bathroom and stared at him

"What?" Miguel asked, feeling a little embarrassed.

"What's going on with you, Peanut? You're acting different," said Benji.

"Oh, I'm fine, just fine. This house is trying to kill me, but everything is fine with me," Miguel said, turning around and sitting on the bed.

Benji walked around to face Miguel. "This doesn't seem very fine."

Miguel looked up and saw the sincere concern in Benji's brown eyes and wanted so badly to be held and feel safe again. "Listen, I am having a really hard time right now."

Benji took a seat by Miguel and rested his arm over his shoulder, "Talk to me; what's going on?"

"You're going to think I'm insane." Miguel turned away.

"I'm used to crazy; I'm married to you."

Miguel gave Benji a look, but not the smile he knew he wanted,

"Okay. I'm seriously getting worried now."

Miguel stood up and began to pace, "Fine, I'll tell you, okay? You're not going to believe me because why would you? But I'm going to tell you anyway."

"I'm ready."

"I think this house is haunted," Miguel said as he stopped in place and faced Benji.

Benji first looked confused, then began laughing. "Haunted? Miguel, I thought something was seriously wrong."

"Something is seriously wrong! It's this place! Day after day, something new seems to happen, and I'm running out of excuses for why."

"You are overwhelmed. There's been a lot of change, and it's clearly affecting you."

Miguel was offended. "NO! What's affecting me is the doors slamming for no reason, locking our kid in the cellar, and some shadow of a man disappearing right before my eyes."

"Okay. Slow down; you're making no sense now. When did all that happen?"

"Today, Benji! When I busted my face trying to break down the damn door that, by the way, doesn't even have a lock!"

"You hit your head?" Benji asked as he rose and grabbed a medical kit from the closet. "I thought you just bumped your nose on something."

"Yeah, I did. When that hard door slammed in my face."

Benji pulled out a flashlight and pointed it at Miguel.

"Stop that," Miguel said, swatting the flashlight away.

"You should have called the clinic; I would come home."

"I was more concerned about Brandy-Sue trying to call an exorcist and keeping an eye on Wyatt!"

"So you hit your head, and you saw something that is perfectly natural."

"I don't need a doctor right now. I need my husband! It's not the first time something like that has happened in this house."

"Listen, we've been through a lot of changes the last few months. You're trapped in this house, focusing on every creak and noise that it makes. You've worked yourself up to the point where you think the impossible is happening."

"I wish you would actually listen to me."

"I am!"

"NO! You are responding, but you think I'm crazy, and you won't even try to trust me on this!"

That last statement hung in the air for a while before Benji walked over to Miguel again and said, "I'm sorry, I'm sorry. Seriously, I haven't been considering what it must feel like being couped up in here like this. I've been so focused at work we've lost touch with each other." Miguel lowered his defenses and allowed Benji to hold him again. "I think we need to do something about that."

"Like what?" Miguel asked.

"Let's take a trip again to the city, you and me. We can let Gideon watch the kids for a weekend and have Mary check in on them."

Miguel felt a burst of excitement, but the feeling was followed by guilt. "But the house."

"This house is old and rundown, nothing more. No one else has had any problems." Benji pulled away for a moment to look into Miguel's eyes with a stern look, "We need this. I'm run down here. Work has taken a lot out of me." Miguel knew Benji was right, at least for the most part. He couldn't explain what he saw, but maybe it was just from an overworked mind.

"Okay, maybe you're right, but the last time we left Gideon in charge, all three kids were running around outside."

"I'm sure Gideon learned his lesson. We need to give him a chance to redeem himself and don't forget, Mary will be here often."

They agreed, and Benji walked back to the closet to put his medical bag away. When he was out of sight, Miguel quickly checked under the bed one last time.

Chapter 26

It was the day of the festival, and Miguel and Benji had already left for their trip. Emma lay on her bed staring at the doll Miguel had given her. There was something weird about the way it stared at her, so she got up and threw a blanket over its head. It had been a couple hours since Miguel and Benji said their goodbyes and gave them all stern talks about responsibilities and blah, blah. *Now would be a great time for something exciting to happen with the case*, Emma thought to herself. But nope! No luck, just a boring evening spent bothering Gideon for updates. She decided to go downstairs and get another update. It had been a whole twenty minutes since the last one. Emma walked outside of her room and saw that Wyatt was sitting at Uncle Benji's door, with his head between his legs and his left hand tapping his brace.

"Whatcha doing there, kiddo?"

Wyatt didn't raise his head. "Nothing."

"Doesn't look like nothing."

Wyatt looked up, and Emma could tell from his puffy eyes that he had been crying.

"Okay, are you missing them?" Emma walked over and sat next to him. "They just left for a couple of days, you know? They are going to come back."

"Mom and Dad not back."

Emma took a moment to swallow the pain that statement reopened. Her voice cracked as she first attempted to reply. She took another breath and cleared her throat. "Come on. Let's get some cereal, okay?" Wyatt shook his head and wiped away some new tears that had formed. They got up together, and Emma helped him down the stairs. Once they reached the kitchen, an annoyed Gideon turned to her.

"Listen, I'm going to tell you what I said twenty minutes ago. We're not going yet. I'll tell you when." Gideon stopped as he noticed Wyatt next to her.

"Can you help us get some cereal?" Emma asked.

"Yeah, yeah, cereal sounds great." The three of them sat together in the dining area and ate their fill of sugary flakes. Emma thought about how Miguel had always forced them all to eat together every night. At the time, she had found it kind of annoying, but now, with just the three of them, it felt emptier and lacked the color and silliness that the uncles brought every night.

"I miss Miguel," Wyatt said, stirring his spoon in the soggy cereal.

"Uh yeah, I miss Miguel too," Gideon replied halfheartedly. "He's a funny guy."

"Remember when Miguel got mad at Uncle Benji because he kept forgetting to close the front door properly when we went out to town?" Emma asked.

"Yeah. Miguel raced up to the front door and closed it ten times in front of us and then said, 'You see how easy that is?' He stood there and waited until Benji showed him he could do it." They all burst out in laughter, and Wyatt fell over, spilling his bowl, causing them to erupt into even more laughter.

Ring, ring. The sound of the telephone created a silence between the three as they looked at each other with concern. Emma watched as Gideon got up to answer the phone. "Okay, you're on your way? Great. We will be ready." As Gideon hung up, he motioned to Emma to follow. As they walked into the foyer, they grabbed their jackets and stopped.

"Where are we going?" Wyatt asked as he attempted to put his jacket on.

"What do we do about him?" Emma asked in a hushed tone. Before Gideon could think of an answer, Mary popped her head in from Grandpa's room.

"Hey, you guys. Is everything alright? I heard the phone."

"Yes! Great, amazing even. In fact, Agi is actually on her way to pick us up," Gideon said.

"Oh, that sounds nice."

"Yes, very nice and very safe," Emma added.

"Okay, well, I hope you all have fun."

Emma turned to Wyatt. "You can't come with us. We need you to stay and watch the house."

"Pants on fire!"

"Wyatt, please, we have to go."

"Pants. On. Fire!" Wyatt stomped off.

"We're coming right back," Emma shouted after him.

Emma and Gideon went to the front door. As Gideon was opening it, Emma looked back at Grandpa's room. She saw Grandpa Emory looking right at them via his mirror with a Cheshire Cat smile that sent shivers through her body. She shook it off and ran outside behind Gideon, who was waiting on the porch for Agatha. A few minutes passed until the low beams of her car pulled in. They rushed into the vehicle with the motor still running, and Agatha stepped on the gas.

Chapter 27

They pulled into town. Above the narrow cobblestone road hung orange and brown garlands. People were already walking to booths that were scattered about the area. Gideon had never seen so many pumpkins of all colors and sizes. Some were painted, some carved, and one even stood as tall as Emma. They parked in a spot near the big boot, and before they opened a door, the smell of funnel cake and hay wafted into the car. "Is that a horse?" Emma asked. Gideon glanced over to see a team of horses pulling a wagon with a small group of people on it. Somewhere in the distance was the faint sound of a band playing, which was disrupted by a loud buzzer.

"Ring toss," Miles said. His eyes lit up.

"Maybe we should split up and cover more ground," Gideon suggested.

Without another word, Miles, Emma, and Channing rushed away toward the games. Agatha gave Gideon a grin, and they walked further into the festival. They came closer to the live music, which was played by some of the town's people on a combination of fiddles, guitars, drums, and one old timer with an accordion. Gideon didn't usually find this kind of music that exciting, but in the setting of this small-town festival, it made him feel like dancing.

"Don't look now, but there's the mayor and Sheriff Colon," Agatha said. Gideon spun around and saw Spruce standing with her usual scowl as she watched people. Her gaze shifted to them, and she leaned over to whisper something to the Sheriff. Her gazing at Gideon made him feel uneasy. Suddenly, he noticed Colin moving toward them.

"Oh crap, he is coming over here," Agatha said.

"Well, how about a dance?" Gideon asked with his hand extended. Agatha looked at him. Her face was red, but she took his hand and followed him toward the stage. A few older couples were dancing, and Gideon relaxed into it as he began to sway with her to the lively folk music. Some of the other dancers took notice of them. One older man grinned and wiggled his eyebrows. Gideon turned away and found himself looking right into Agatha's eyes. No words came out, but he thought to himself how beautiful she was, with strands of hair falling from her ponytail across her worried brow. Her red crystal shined brighter than usual.

She turned her face from him. "I can't see him anymore."

"I guess we are good, then."

"Yeah." She stopped dancing. "Let's go over there for a moment."

Gideon followed her over to a bench that had a scarecrow on either side of it. A small maze made with stacks of hay was behind it, which children wiggled their way through. They sat down together.

"Are you okay?" Gideon asked.

Agatha played with the crystal around her neck. "You probably think it's strange that I know so much about this stuff. I didn't really want to bring it up in front of the others, but I feel like you understand."

"Yeah, you can tell me anything, Agi."

She looked up at him, "My mom and I, we've lived here my whole life. But my dad used to live here with us, too. He disappeared when I was really young, though."

"Oh, I'm sorry to hear that."

"Well, people believe he abandoned us, but that's not true. He was a loving father and husband. He would never have done that." Agatha was getting choked up, and her words stumbled over each other.

Gideon put his hand on her back and scooted closer. He had a strong urge to comfort her. "Hey, I believe you. I have no reason not to."

She gave him a rueful smile. "I appreciate that. I know what happened to him. Others went missing like him, and now the same thing is happening again. My mom and I need closure."

"So, you saw the exact same signs in your dad before he disappeared?"

"Yes. I just don't know why this is happening." She looked down at her hands.

Gideon took her hands into his and waited for her to look up at him, "You aren't alone with this anymore. I won't stop until we figure it out together." They held each other's gaze, and Gideon noticed her lean closer to him. He found himself leaning closer as well. They were hardly an inch away from each other.

"You buffoon!" A familiar voice shouted, "Who taught you how to throw a dart? Ya damn blind goat."

Gideon jerked his head away to see Carl and Roy standing near one of the game booths.

"I throw better than you ever did, Carl!"

"You could throw them at me from where you're standing and still miss!"

"Something the matter?" Agatha asked, pulling away from Gideon.

"Yeah, just saw something, sorry," Gideon said, a little embarrassed. They sat there quietly. *Caw.* "You say something?" Gideon asked.

"Are you serious? That was obviously a crow." Agatha stood up instantly.

"Oh right, sorry, I knew that. I just…"

"Shush! Gideon, that was a crow! Where did the sound come from?"

Realizing what she meant, Gideon stood up as well. " I think I heard it flying somewhere over there." He pointed to some trees near the edge of town. They rushed over and saw a family standing under one of the enormous trees.

"Robert, you are acting strange again," a slender woman with short hair said.

"I'm fine, dear. Really. Don't let this little fainting spell stop you and the kids from having fun."

"I think we should head home now." The three kids began yelling and complaining about leaving.

"We wanna do the cakewalk." One of them pouted.

"Go ahead, but don't go too far," the man said. All three kids took off toward a booth with a group of people walking in a circle. Music blared from a speaker behind them. There was a stand beside it with a variety of baked goods. A plump lady laughed into a microphone as the music stopped, and everyone rushed to stand on an orange circle. Two people were left without a circle to stand on.

"You're out," she half yelled, half laughed.

That was when Gideon saw them. Miles, Emma, and Channing were walking in the circle, bobbing to the music. Gideon shook his head. "It looks like it's up to us." He turned back to see the man and woman headed over to watch their kids. "Do you know who they are?"

"Yes, that's the Allen family. They moved here a couple of years ago."

"Good intentions only get you so far," Spruce said from behind Agatha and Gideon. They both jumped back and turned to face her.

"Again, I find you children sneaking around and getting yourselves in over your heads."

"You can't keep letting this happen," Agatha shouted.

"Letting what happen?" Spruce replied.

"Don't try to deny what's happening here," Agatha said. Gideon grabbed her arm and pulled her closer to him.

"And what is happening here, Miss Beckett? What do you really think is happening? You have but a grain of sand compared to an entire desert. Go back to your mother, child."

"Let's go, Agi, she isn't worth it." Gideon pulled Agatha away, and she followed. He turned and saw Mayor Spruce watching.

Once they were a good distance away, Agatha stopped. "She knows we are on to her."

"It doesn't matter if she knows or not. We have to keep our cool and watch the Allen family." Miles, Emma, and Channing ran up to them, eating cupcakes. "Hey guys! How goes the search?" Miles asked, with cupcakes smeared all over his face.

"Clearly not as good as yours," Gideon replied. Guys, we think we have located the next victim."

"That's great," Emma said with her mouth full.

"Yeah, it's Robert Allen over there." Agatha pointed, and everyone turned to look, but the Allen family had left. "Oh crap, where did they go?"

"The Allen family? I think I saw them walk off toward the parked cars," Miles said. "They were probably heading home."

"Do either of you know where they live?" Gideon asked.

"Oh, for sure, dude! I pass by their place on the way to school almost every day."

"Alright, great, let's head back to the van. We need to go there." Gideon turned to check on Mayor Spruce one last time, but she was gone.

Chapter 28

After some time on the road and as the day finished setting, they reached the Allen's residence. There was a single squad car out front without its lights on. It was a small house with a picket fence. Emma thought it looked like one of those houses from a black-and-white TV show. It had bushes out front and a stone path leading to the door. But instead of the perfect family smiling and waving, a mom was holding a baby in her nightgown and yelling at the sheriff, who was taking notes. Two other kids about Emma's age or younger were crying while tugging at their mom. When they parked, Miles got out first.

"Why is the Sheriff here?" Miles asked.

"I'm not sure, but he is going to make this a lot more difficult," Gideon said.

The group snuck over to the squad car to try and listen in. The sheriff spoke in hushed tones while Mrs. Allen talked loudly enough to be heard over the kids' cries.

"Why hasn't anyone done anything yet?" Mrs. Allen yelled.

"It takes time to put together a search party, ma'am. We don't want people running into those woods alone."

"My husband is out there alone, and you have just been standing there writing nonsense on your little notepad."

"I'm just doing my job. Your husband wasn't kidnapped; he simply walked in there by choice."

"There was no choice! We were eating dinner when he started acting as if he was possessed. I couldn't even pull him back inside."

"Did he have anything to drink?"

Emma, who heard everything, couldn't stop herself from going around the car and rushing up to them.

"Emma, no," Gideon said to stop her. When he realized it was too late, the rest of them stood up and followed.

Emma marched up to the sheriff, who was already visibly annoyed. "He wasn't drunk; the woods took him!"

"Excuse me, young lady? Where are your parents?"

"Mrs. Allen isn't lying," Agatha said, coming up behind them.

Collin looked over to see the rest of them, "What the….what is this? Some sort of game you kids are playing? Go home!"

Miles rushed up next to Agatha and said, "Sheriff, sir, um, seriously, things aren't right here. I mean, we've been following this family."

"I'm sorry. You've been what?" The sheriff suddenly went from confused to angry. His eyes almost looked wild as he looked around at everyone, "I think I'm going to need to bring all of you down to the station." The sheriff, surrounded by a yelling mom and panicked teens, tried his best to make everyone calm down. Emma stepped back, watching the scene play out. Her eyes were drawn to the two kids crying next to their mom. One of them was sobbing into her dress while the other one kept pulling on her arm.

"Where did Dad go?" the child asked.

Emma couldn't hear anything else as she felt the pain and fear of losing her own parents the same way they were losing theirs. At that moment, nothing else mattered. Only a single thought drove her mind. *Save him.* She turned around and took off at a full sprint, heading to the back of the house.

"Where is she going?" yelled the sheriff.

Before reaching the edge of the woodline, Emma heard Gideon's voice.

"Emma!"

She did not turn around or slow down for a moment, rushing directly over the leaves, stirring them up in her wake. She scanned the ground for clues, but it was already dark, and the footprints were most likely covered by leaves. So, she just kept running in the general direction, hoping something would show her the way. For a moment, she became scared; she was just getting more lost in the woods and prayed for some sort of sign. Her prayers were answered, at least she hoped, in the form of a glowing light far in the distance. She couldn't be sure, but she felt a similar warmth to that she had felt when surrounded by the dancing, glowing orbs of light. She took a hard right turn and chased after it. Whenever she felt she was getting close enough to see it in detail, the light reappeared further away. She continued to follow, trying her best to make plenty of noise so her brother could keep pace. Eventually, one light turned to two like small glowing eyes staring back at her. She could still hear the others yelling her name behind her, but she now heard a new sound. The sound of crunching leaves in front of her. She was gaining on him. She put whatever she had left into her burning legs. The lights, instead of fading, became brighter and brighter as she ran full speed toward them. *Screeech.* Her body stopped, frozen, as she realized she was running straight into that car again. She braced. *Crash.*

Emma heard screaming, but it was dark. She floated in a sea of blackness, feeling all the cuts and tears she had endured on the fatal day of the car accident. Her chest felt heavy, and she was unable to will her body to move. Her heartbeat matched the single beep of a hospital monitor. The pressure felt massive. For a moment, she was sure death had finally taken her.

"Emma!" In the dark, she could hear the faint whisper of her name; it felt familiar. "Emma. I got you." She heard the voice again; it sounded like her dad, but maybe not. As she tried to place it, she felt her body suddenly jerk up and rise. The heaviness subsided. "I got you, Emma!" The voice came through louder. It wasn't her dad; it was her brother. She was not lost anymore. Her brother had found her. As she remembered where she was, her sight returned, and she looked up to see Gideon, who was in a full sprint toward the stones that were now in her view.

Emma's eyes focused on the scene playing out in front of them. Mr. Allen was standing in the middle of the stone circle. Directly behind him towered a very pale-looking woman with beat red eyes. Her fingers were like sharp claws hanging from bony, long arms. Emma looked around for a moment and saw that Miles and Agatha were right next to Gideon. They were all charging toward the stones.

"What do we do when we get there?" Miles asked

"No idea, man, we just have to get there," Gideon replied.

"We need to hurry before she takes him," said Agatha.

Emma knew Agatha was right, but she could never have imagined such a surreal sight. The creature was beyond anything she ever thought possible. However, despite the fear, she felt a strange pity for it without knowing why. As they got closer, the banshee, who was as still as the stones around her, finally took notice of them. Her red eyes darted around, and she opened her unnaturally elongated mouth.

A high-pitched sound came out, causing Emma to clutch her ears in agonizing pain. Her eardrums vibrated, feeling like they were about to explode. Suddenly, she felt herself slip from Gideon's arms. Her back slammed against the ground, knocking the wind out of her. She turned to see Gideon on his knees, holding his ears as well. Then, she could see Miles and Agatha doing the same. For a moment, everything went dark again. Then the scream stopped. Emma opened her eyes, and a loud ringing inside her head replaced the creature's screeching. She could not hear anything, and from what she could tell, neither could anyone else. Emma looked over at the stones again. She was still on her back and was surprised to see that both Mr. Allen and the creature had vanished. As she lifted herself back up, rubbing her ears, she made her way over to the stones. The rest of them followed. Emma looked up and noticed that a once blank stone now had a bright red symbol etched into it.

"We were too late," Emma said, but she could hardly hear her own voice.

Chapter 29

Gideon was the first one to make it to the porch. He turned around to see his friends looking beaten and defeated. He looked at Emma and saw she had been crying again.

"C'mon guys; let's get some food and rest for a bit. We can figure out what to do next afterward." No one responded, possibly due to the ringing in their ears and from what they had just experienced. When they entered the house, they were immediately greeted by a worried Mary. She grabbed Agatha and looked her up and down.

"You all look like you've been through a war. What happened?" They looked at each other, unsure how to answer a seemingly simple question. "Well? Is anyone going to speak up?"

"Mom, I think everyone needs something to eat."

For a moment, Mary looked at them and then seemed to relax her posture. "Well, I don't know what y'all were up to, but I guess I'm just glad everyone got home in one piece." She paused for a second before letting out a deep sigh and beckoning them to follow her into the kitchen. They made it into the hallway, and then she said, "Look. I'll warm up something on the stove; you guys just try and get cl..." Before she could finish her sentence, she jerked back as if someone had punched her right in the stomach. She looked up in confusion before flying backward and disappearing into the darkness of the cellar behind her. The cellar door slammed while Agatha was racing to reach it. Her fist slammed on the door as she tried desperately to open it.

"Mom! Mom!" Agatha yelled. She turned to Gideon with fear-stricken eyes. "Help me!" Gideon was rushing to help her push the door when he heard the sound of shattering glass from the front parlor. Instinctively, he darted toward the sound with Emma, Miles, and Channing just behind him. When he reached the room, he froze in the doorway. Glass littered the floor with no sign of anything having come through the window.

"What the hell is going on?" Miles asked.

"It has to be that creature," Gideon replied.

They could still hear Agatha banging and struggling to get to her mother. Out of the corner of his eye, Gideon caught sight of Grandpa's door opening slowly. Its hinges creaked, and the dark shadow from inside the room grew into the hall. The hair on Gideon's arms rose. Before he had a chance to react, a low rattling sound from the kitchen caught his attention. It started off as a hum and developed into loud clanking. Gideon turned to see the pots and pans over the island banging into one another. He crept toward the kitchen, noticing the cabinets shaking and their doors slowly opening. It was as if an earthquake was happening in that one room. A large pot hit the island and clanked onto the floor, causing Miles to jump. One after another, pots and pans fell, hitting the island and bouncing off onto the floor. The cabinets continued to shake and started spilling out their contents of bowls and plates, which shattered against the tiled floor.

"What is happening?" Channing screamed. Agatha screamed from the cellar door. Gideon charged to meet her, only to see her staring wildly in his direction.

"Your, your grandpa. He was just standing right there."

146

"My grandpa can't stand on his own two legs, Agi; what are you talking about?"

"He was right there, smiling at me."

They all rushed to Grandpa Emory's open door only to see an empty wheelchair.

Miles began to hyperventilate, "Oh my god, oh my God, I should have gone home."

Thump. A loud noise came from upstairs.

Thump. Thump. It got progressively faster and faster.

Emma reached the stairs first and looked up. "I think that's my room!" She raced upstairs.

"Dammit, Emma!" Gideon yelled after her. They all ran upstairs, and as they reached the top of the stairs, the house fell silent. "Emma," Gideon whispered down the unlit hallway. They moved slowly forward. "Emma?" Gideon said a little louder. She poked her head into the hallway from her room.

"I'm right here!" She went back into her room, and they all filed in after her.

Miles was the last one in. "We should be leaving the house, not going deeper into it."

"Not until we figure this out," Agatha replied.

"Guys, everything in my room has moved," Emma said in a low voice. Her eyes were wide, glancing around toward each dark corner as if someone might pop out at her at any moment. Gideon scanned the room, not knowing what it originally looked like. The bed was in the center of the room, with the doll Miguel had bought Emma sitting on it. It didn't seem too out of the ordinary until his eyes were drawn to the sea of white fluff all over the floor, mixed with the ripped-apart bodies of stuffed animals. He noticed Emma holding one, a small gorilla with a bowtie that had its head ripped off.

"Mom gave me this one," Emma said.

"Emma," the cheery voice of the doll exclaimed from the bed. "Emma," it repeated. "Emma, Emma, Emma, Emma." It continued to repeat as its voice got deeper in a way that made it sound menacing, and the word Emma started to warp. "Emma, Emma, Emma, Emma! EMMA!"

***

Crash.

Wyatt's eyes opened as he woke up in a fog of sleep. Confused, he rubbed his eyes and sat up in bed. He could have sworn he had heard something in the hall. He placed his little feet on the ground, limped slowly to the door, and tried to listen to what was happening outside of it. He thought he heard his sister's doll say "Emma." Curious, he opened his door slowly and peeked outside of it. As he turned to look, he saw the tall figure of a man standing at the end of the hallway. At first, he didn't recognize him, but then, as his sleepy eyes adjusted, he realized who it was. "Grandpa?"

Grandpa Emory, facing the other direction, dropped his head down, twisted his back, and stared at Wyatt with a smile that stretched to his ears. "I'm so tired of being trapped. Can you free me, Wyatt?" Wyatt ran back into his room and slammed his door. His little body quivered as he rushed to hide under the bed. Panic set in, and his breathing quickened. He tried his best to be silent as he heard footstep after footstep walking closer to his door. When they reached his door, there was a pause before the knob slowly began to turn open. The door eased open, and he could see his grandpa's bare feet standing in the doorway.

Grandpa walked a few steps into the room, and Wyatt held his mouth closed, trying to be as quiet as possible, but his heartbeat was loud in his ears. He was sure it would betray him. Emory then turned around and walked slowly out of the room. Wyatt listened to him walking further away and carefully down the steps. He took a breath of air, thinking it was over. The moment was short-lived as suddenly Wyatt could hear Grandpa sprinting back up the stairs, through the hall, and into Wyatt's room again. This time, Granpa's feet stopped right at the side of the bed. Wyatt began to weep as fear overtook him; he felt a wet warmth spread down his leg. He watched as Grandpa lifted himself onto the bed. Wyatt felt the springs dip down, almost touching him; he could tell that Grandpa Emory was sitting right above him.

"I'm so tired, Wyatt. Why won't you free me?" An old, shriveled hand grasped the bottom of the bed. Wyatt's eyes grew wild with terror. "They trapped me, Wyatt, trapped me in stones like Grandpa in that little wheelchair." A second shriveled hand grasped the bottom of the bed. Wyatt's breathing became uncontrollable. Grandpa's head lowered unnaturally fast, staring right at Wyatt. "Free me now!"

***

Miles turned to Gideon after tossing the doll into the closet and shutting the door. "Let's promise to throw that thing in a bonfire filled with sage later, okay?" A loud scream from Wyatt's room caused everyone to turn around and face the door. The group immediately rushed out into the hall to see what had happened.

When Gideon reached the doorway, he saw an empty bed. "Wyatt? Are you in here?" A whimpering emanated from under the bed. Gideon walked over and knelt down, seeing Wyatt in the fetal position. He reached out his hand and pulled him out from underneath the bed. Gideon lifted Wyatt up and carried him out of the room as the rest followed. "We need to get out of this house." He felt the fabric of

Wyatt's pajamas damp against his arm. He smelled the distinct odor of urine. "I'll get you out of here, buddy," he whispered to his brother. They made their way down the stairs, noticing more things had moved from their original places. Gideon grabbed the handle of the front door and gave it a tug, but it refused to budge. He tried again, but still nothing.

"What are you doing? We have to get my mom," said Agatha.

"After I get Wyatt out of here," Gideon replied

"There's a perfectly good broken window," Miles added.

Before a plan could be decided on, Gideon felt a sticky, wet substance dripping from above him and down his neck. He slowly looked up and let out a gasp as he realized the liquid was drool dripping out of his grandpa's smiling mouth. Grandpa was hanging off the ceiling like a bat when the rest of the group noticed a mixture of screams and swearing followed. Gideon just stared right into Grandpa's wild eyes.

"Trapped! All of you are trapped just like me," Emory screamed down to them.

Wyatt tightened his grip on Gideon, his nails digging into his arm. "Who are you?"

Emory let out a wheezy laugh. "Inevitable." His head whipped violently to the side, producing a crunching noise that ended in a pop. Then his eyes glossed over, the smile relaxed, and his body flew down to the floor, making a tremendous thud against the hardwood. No one screamed or reacted; they just stood there in silence, half expecting the mangled body to stand back up.

A loud bang at the front door shook them all out of it. Things continued to fly around in every room, and lights flickered on and off. There was another bang at the door. Gideon felt helpless. He could not figure out how to react as a third bang, louder than the others, came from the other side of the doorway. A final boom threw the doors open, and a light emanated from outside as a thunderous voice chanted in a language unknown to Gideon. As he tried to look at what was producing the light, he thought he could make out the antlers of a giant stag attached to a human body. As the light dissipated, the image of the stag receded, and stood in its place was Mayor Spruce, holding out one hand and continuously chanting in a foreign tongue. Things in the manor began to stop moving, and the lights stopped flickering as she moved further inside. In one final moment, she yelled out with both arms raised, and as she let her arms drop, the house seemed to stop trembling. As she finished, the sheriff came walking up behind her with his revolver out, looking around.

"Oh, put that thing away, Collins; everything is settled now."

"Oh, uh, yes, ma'am."

Spruce looked at Gideon and the rest. As they stared in utter disbelief, she looked down and saw the body of Grandpa Emory on the ground, "Oh dear, I am so sorry. Now, I guess there is no going back."

"What the hell is going on, Mayor Spruce?" Gideon yelled.

She shook her head, still staring at Emory's body, before giving a quick backward glance at Sheriff Collins. "We need to take care of this right away, Sheriff."

"Yes, ma'am," he replied.

"Not until you tell us what's going on. My grandpa is dead!" Gideon said.

"And what about my mom? She's still stuck in the cellar," Agatha added.

"You kids have no idea what you've been meddling in," Mayor Spruce said. "This house has a dark history, one that involves your family, Gideon. It has for generations."

"And it took someone dying for you to say anything about it?" Gideon said through gritted teeth.

"Watch your tone, boy; you're talking to a high druid," Collins announced

"High druid?" Emma said to herself quietly.

Spruce shot a look at Collins that made him quickly look down like a dog in trouble, "There are more complex things at work here, and I don't have time to explain them all."

"Okay yeah, but that's bullshit," Miles said. Spruce's eyes widened as if she had never been more disrespected, "Give us the Cliff notes."

"You should watch your mouth, Miles. I knew both your mom and her mom when they were in diapers!" She calmed down before adding, "But fine, I can tell you that all of this is connected to the founder, this town, and the victims. It is a sacred ritual that was made to keep a great evil from permeating into our reality once more."

"So this ritual is why people have to go missing? To feed into some religious nonsense?" Agatha asked.

"It is not religious nonsense, young lady; it is an ancient power that has existed since before humans. You would do well to respect it."

"Yeah, right, so this ancient power waits years to take innocent people from their homes and families!" Gideon could tell that Agatha was becoming even more aggressive with her questions. All of this had hit her on a personal level.

"I know you are angry after what you've been through with your dad, Agatha."

"You don't know half of what I've been through, lady!"

"We deserve answers," Miles added.

"What do you know about my family?" asked Gideon.

"Enough!" Spruce's voice thundered through the house, her presence consuming the whole space and causing everyone else to fall silent. "I will tell you enough so that maybe you will stop acting like children and respond appropriately.

"We are children," Emma retorted

The mayor let out a long sigh and then continued. "Before this town came under my protection…." Agatha sneered….. "there were dealings with an evil magic that resulted in a ritual being formed." Mayor Spruce walked over to the staircase. "This ritual was because of a mistake that your ancestors made. A mistake that cost a young woman's life and bound her soul to this place." Spruce rubbed her hand on the banister, almost as if she was recalling her own memories. "None of that is important now. What is important is that you young ones stop getting in the way of something you do not understand." She looked over at the group, "If this ritual fails, more than a few lives will be lost; the entire town will be in great peril." As she finished, she walked over to Grandpa Emory, knelt down, and waved her hand over his body, "HE is no longer possessed and may rest." She then grabbed his head and, with a loud crack, snapped his neck back into place. She then waved her hand over his body once more and spoke in that same odd language. Emory's wounds disappeared, and he almost looked as if he was in a peaceful sleep.

"What are those words you keep speaking?" Emma asked.

The druid looked up at her and smiled at Emma's curiosity. "It is Gaelic. The language from where I was born." The mayor stood back up. "Right, so I am going to head to the cellar to make sure Mary is fine. Collins, take Grandpa Emory and put him back in bed. Stop standing there and make yourself useful!" At that, Collins rushed over, carefully lifted Emory up, and placed him back in his room in bed.

Gideon stood there for a while, unable to look at anyone, feeling truly disturbed at learning that his family had a part in all of this. After several minutes, Spruce walked back into the foyer with Mary, who looked confused and was rubbing her head.

"So, I called 911 but didn't get a response," said Mary.

"That's right, dear. Emory was old, and his time came. You did everything right," Spruce replied.

"Oh, oh no, Gideon, Emma, I am so sorry this happened. I guess I passed out with everything happening with your Grandpa?"

"It's fine, Mary. Thank you for making Grandpa's last moments comfortable," Gideon said as a flash of Emory's mangled body went across his mind. Agatha ran to her mom, and they embraced, crying. As people started filtering out of the house, Gideon had almost forgotten he was holding Wyatt, who had fallen asleep. He walked back upstairs and put him back in bed. Emma followed, and they all slept in Wyatt's room with the door locked.

Chapter 30

The sunrise looked like a perfect watercolor painting, sending warm rays of sunlight that spotted the ground. Birds sang, flying from tree to tree, and the smell of freshly stirred soil lingered in the air. It was the promise of a beautiful day. Emma watched as a blue-speckled butterfly fluttered onto the glossy red-brown coffin. Someone from the back of the small crowd sniffled, and she felt Wyatt shift closer to her.

"The souls of men are immortal, and as he ends his journey through this life, Emory takes with him the love from those close, into the next where he may live again." The Mayor spoke loudly, in a solemn tone. The tone was the same, Emma thought, but the scene was very different. At her mother and father's funeral, the priest was a stuffy fat man with a red face and white collar who read from the bible in a monotone voice. Here, the mayor spoke in a way that captured the attention of everyone. It made her want to believe. Mary, who was a few feet behind her, cried and dabbed at her face with a tissue, clutching Agatha's arm. Gideon glanced back at Agatha, and Emma noticed her avert her eyes, fixing her gaze on a spot on the ground. Gideon frowned and looked ahead as Mayor Spruce continued speaking.

"But let us only grieve a bit longer for Emory. Let us not feel sunk by death and instead revel in life and all it still promises! This is how we may defeat death and celebrate this man's great legacy!" She finished, and what followed was the melancholy sound of a fiddle being played as a few men stood up with rounded stones in hand. The casket began to lower, and one by one, different people walked over and placed their stones around the grave. Emma could barely recognize Sheriff Collin, who had shaved and put on a tight-fitting suit. It had probably not seen use in years. He pulled on his collar a few times before placing his stone and turning around. Behind him stood Mary with tears streaming down her face. She walked with her stone close to her chest and Agatha holding her arm. When she placed her stone beside the grave, she knelt down a moment, and Emma could hear as she muttered, "I'm sorry."

A few more people from the town went up and placed their stones until there was only one stone missing from the circle. Emma turned to Benji and saw in his face an expression that could have been seen as cold and distant but, if viewed a little longer, would reveal a man who went inward when feeling deep sorrow. Miguel nudged him to stand and followed suit. They walked together arm in arm until they reached the spot in the circle where they were meant to complete it. Emma sat transfixed on him. She wondered if her uncle/dad knew the truth, would he be angry with her and not let her live with him anymore. As he put his final stone down, the fiddle switched to a faster and brighter tune. The mayor knelt and picked up a handful of dirt, whispered something, and threw it into the hole where Emma's grandpa would stay forever.

After the funeral, everyone was led to a small building near the graveyard. Inside was a table that had little sandwiches and cups of coffee. Emma made her way to the back, where Gideon and Agatha were speaking in hushed tones.

"I just, I just don't know what you are thinking," Agatha said

"I was thinking we need to do what the mayor said and let this thing be," Gideon replied.

"So let more people die?" Agatha looked visibly upset.

Gideon shrugged, "This thing is way more complicated than any of us understand. I just think that we need to keep our heads down and try to get back to a normal life."

"I'm sure that all the victims would have liked to return to a normal life."

"Agatha, please."

"Maybe I would have liked to have had a normal life." She turned away, and Emma thought she might cry.

Gideon felt shame come over him as he remembered what Agatha had told him about her father. "I'm sorry, Agi; I'm not trying to be insensitive." He moved closer.

Agatha looked up at him for a moment as if to decide whether to say something before taking a deep breath. "Now that I know about the ritual…"

"It doesn't exactly bring closure."

"Right. My mom and I have been through a lot together. My dad, well, I don't really remember him, but I remember how he affected my mother. She took years to recover from his disappearance." Emma felt herself pulled in as she heard all this, walking closer to hear everything Agatha was saying.

"My dad vanished, and it was treated as if he just decided one day to up and run, but my mom did not accept that. She couldn't believe he was that much of a coward. She spent years trying to convince the sheriff to investigate it further, but he downright refused. He wouldn't even take a statement. Everyone was just fine with taking my dad's name and throwing it in the gutter. And you know what? For a while, I just accepted it. Maybe he did leave us, but why the hell didn't they try to help us find him?"

"Do you really believe your dad was a sacrifice?" Gideon asked.

Agatha raised her head as she breathed in the tears. "Well, honestly, I didn't figure that part out until recently. Not until I started hanging around you. But the timeline works out perfectly, and all the symptoms my mom told me he had before he vanished check out. You know, honestly, this town and me treated her like crap. I thought she was just lying to herself."

"So now you know what happened, what?"

She gave Gideon a sharp look. "We stop it."

"The mayor said it would get worse, more people would die."

"Why are we even believing her?"

"Keep it down."

"I'm serious! Why do we even feel like we can trust that old witch?

"She seems to know a lot more than we do; she fixed my house and helped with Grandpa."

"She covered up a murder."

"Yeah, well, it's kind of hard to explain how a house can kill someone."

"You are unbelievable."

"What do you want from me? We don't even know how to stop it."

"Fine, Gideon. If you just want to pretend that everything is back to normal and this thing is over, then go ahead." Agatha walked away without noticing Emma standing in the hall. As she passed Emma, she whispered, "Coward."

The rest of the event was filled with uncomfortable silences and people Emma didn't know telling her she was in their prayers. When it was finished, the family went back to the manor, and Emma felt a shiver when she looked at her grandpa's empty room.

Chapter 31

It was slightly chilly on the bleachers. Miguel welcomed the warmth on either side of him. He was sandwiched between Emma and Wyatt. He glanced over to see Emma's bright and smiling face. She was focused on the players beating each other up on the field. She winced as they slammed against each other in front of them.

"Awesome!" Emma shouted.

Wyatt, on the other hand, snuggled in closer to him, burrowing his face into Miguel's side. Miguel wrapped an arm around him. This was what it felt like to be a parent. The last week, he had grown to know what that felt like. After the funeral, things around the house changed. There were no longer creepy encounters, and the kids began to truly settle in. They had lively family dinners and even a game night filled with junk food and laughter. The kids stayed up too late, and it all just felt... right.

Miguel was never much of a sports guy, other than some track and field in high school, but watching Gideon on the field made him feel the way others must have felt when their favorite player was on the field. He was invested. Gideon moved faster than Miguel knew possible on ice, weaving and moving the ball through any and all obstacles that tried to block him from the goal. It had been a close game between the Green Hollow Elks and the Boston Bruisers. To say that Gideon was carrying the team was an understatement. Now he had the ball and was making an incredible effort to get it into the net. Miguel didn't remember standing up, but he was fully engaged as Gideon came closer and closer to his target. Two players on the other team charged at Gideon, and it looked as if things were about to go south. Still, amazingly, Gideon, without breaking his stride, knocked the ball between one of their legs, did a full spin, and picked it right back up. The goalie looked as solid as a statue, waiting to try and see what Gideon would do. Gideon raised his stick and, directly before he would have run by the goal, made an angled shot that went into the net past the goalie's right ankle, causing the siren to go off behind him. The whole place erupted into cheering as the game was won with a single point.

"YEEEEEEEESS. That's my boy! He's a champion!" Miguel screamed as his drink fell out of his hand. He didn't even mind the burn his hands endured as he jumped up and down in the stands. "WOOOOOO! Did you see that?" He turned to see most of his family doing the same. Most except his Benji, who was sitting with a glazed-over expression. Miguel leaned over and shook his shoulder until he saw him snap out of whatever trance he was in.

"Benji, You missed Gideon's winning shot."

Benji looked around, confused for a moment, and then rubbed his eyes, "Oh, he scored, that's great. That's awesome." Miguel pulled away and tried to ignore how Benji was acting so he could enjoy the moment Gideon was having.

After the game, they went out for dinner at the brewery. Miguel had a couple drinks after Benji assured him he would be awake enough to drive. Emma told the story of Gideon's awesome win to Miles, who was working concessions and missed the shot. After plenty of laughter and good food, they dropped Miles off and made their way home.

Benji led the way to unlock the door with Gideon carrying Wyatt, who had fallen asleep. Emma bounced along behind him. Miguel shut the doors behind them and paused to take in the eerie glow the mood cast on the house. So much had happened there. Could it all have really been in his head? He shook off those thoughts and started toward the door. From the corner of his eye, a white glow caught his attention. He had to squint, taking a few steps toward the figure before it came into focus. His stomach sank, and a surge of cold ran through him. There in the woodline was the figure of a woman all in white. The same woman Gideon had described.

Chapter 32

The sound of thunder caused Emma to sit up straight. She looked around the room for anything out of the ordinary. Despite the mayor having done something to stop the stuff that happened to the house and killed her grandpa, it was hard to feel safe in the manor. When she was able to confirm to herself that nothing was out of the ordinary, she sighed and lowered her feet from the bed. Nights like this were becoming more and more frequent. Waking up and then not being able to fall back asleep until the sun came up. She looked outside of her room to the dark hallway and checked to make sure things were all clear. She moved toward the stairs to go down to the kitchen. As she got to the stairs, she noticed Benji and Miguel's bedroom door was open. She shrugged it off and started down the stairs. Once she reached the bottom, she went into the parlor connected to the kitchen.

"That song." Emma froze in place when she heard a voice come from the kitchen. It was faint, but she recognized it as a man's voice. "Where's that song coming from?" As she rushed into the kitchen, she realized who the voice belonged to. When she reached the entrance, she saw Benji standing in front of the sink, staring absently out the window. "Uncle Benji? Did the thunder wake you up, too?" Emma asked but got no response. He didn't seem to notice her standing there.

"I think I know this song. Somehow...somehow, I've heard it before."

"What song?"

Benji turned his head, finally noticing Emma, "You hear it too? It's so..." Benji returned to staring out of the window, "So beautiful. It reminds me of..." He trailed off again.

"What does it remind you of?" Emma asked. She got no response again as she stood there, "The song, uncle. What does the song remind you of?"

He turned his head once again, "You hear it too? It's so beautiful." Again, he turned his head back to the window. "I think I've heard it before."

The sound of thunder descended on the house as if it were right above them, causing Emma to scream. She closed her eyes and held her ears until her mind told her it was all right. When she opened her eyes, Benji was on the move, walking up the stairs. Emma rushed to follow. With each step she took, her heart thudded faster and faster. Something wasn't right. Benji slipped back into his room and shut the door. Emma crouched down, resting her head on the floor to see through the small gap beneath the door. There was only darkness, but then she heard the sound of a startled Miguel. The lights flashed on. "Benji? What's going on?" Miguel asked. There was a hint of irritation in his voice, and Emma saw feet hit the floor. After a long stretch of silence, he continued. "Answer me!"

"What?" Benji replied.

"We seriously need to talk. You can't keep doing this; it isn't healthy."

Benji sighed. "I'm sorry I didn't mean to wake you. I'm just overtired and stressed from work."

"No! You can't keep using that excuse. You're having nightmares every night. You're constantly zoning out, and... it's like you aren't even here. Do you know how lonely that is?"

"I promise, I'm just overworked and stressed from the last few weeks."

Emma heard what sounded like a hand smacking the bed. "That's not it! Something isn't right with you, and it's starting to scare me."

"What are you trying to say? I'm losing my mind like my father? I'm in my thirties, Miguel, so my mind should be just fine!"

"Okay, Okay. I'm not saying you are like your dad. I'm not. I'm just saying that something seems off, and it's not just you."

"Please don't say it."

"It's this house. I know a lot of the weird stuff has stopped since we took that trip, but other things seem off."

"Peanut, seriously."

"I saw the same white lady Gideon saw! Nothing about this damn town makes any sense."

"Can we just please go back to sleep? I don't have the energy for this tonight." Emma lifted herself up and raced to Gideon's room to tell him what she heard.

Chapter 33

A crisp breeze rustled the distant trees and caused goosebumps on Gideon's arms. He rubbed at them and continued toward the garden. His eyes were fixed on the lonely statue, the woman whose tears seemed to come to life. His feet kept moving closer despite the anxious feeling that had settled in his chest. It felt like a warning to break his gaze and run back to the house. Before he realized what he was doing, his hand reached out toward the pitiful woman's face, fingers grazing the smooth surface beneath her eyes where a dark gray trickled down her cheeks. Gideon didn't expect to feel the wetness and withdrew his hand to examine his fingers.

When he looked up from his hand, he gasped as he realized that he was suddenly surrounded by trees. Somehow, the statue and he were both planted somewhere in the woods instead of in front of his manor. A sense of dread sank in as he felt lost. That feeling only increased. He swore he saw something within the darkness of the trees staring back at him. With barely a moment to react to what was happening, he saw the silhouette of a woman in ragged white clothes run between the trees on his left. He turned to watch and see if she would reveal herself, but instead, he could hear the sound of something moving behind him. He twisted so fast he felt dizzy. He caught a glimpse of the same tattered woman's leg as she dashed behind another tree. For an agonizing few moments that felt like an eternity, nothing else happened. Gideon kept his back to the statue while moving his eyes in every direction. He didn't need to keep looking, though, because a bright light came from the distance in front of him, slowly revealing more of its form as it came closer and closer. Gideon's eyes widened as he realized it was the white creature from the woodline, but this time, she glowed like some angelic figure. As she grew closer and more of her features were visible, he couldn't help but notice the glint of something emerald green on her wrist.

"Find me." The woman whispered gently in his ear.

Gideon felt drawn closer to examine her, but something snatched at his ankle, sending panic through him. He looked down to see a decaying arm had reached from under the statue and grabbed him. On the bony wrist was that same emerald bracelet. He jolted awake.

Chapter 34

"Gideon… Gideon. Wake up!" He sat up in bed, heart thudding aggressively against his chest. Emma stared back at him with wide, fearful eyes, which did nothing to calm his nerves.

"What is it? What's wrong?"

"It's uncle Benji. I heard him and Miguel talking, and he…." She paused to suck in a deep breath of air. "I think he will be the next victim."

Gideon reached out, putting a hand on each of her shoulders, and leveled his gaze to hers. She was frantic, "Just calm down. Why do you think that? What was said?"

"I saw him in the kitchen, and he wasn't acting right. He kept saying he heard a song. Then I heard Miguel say that he has nightmares and isn't sleeping. He said that it's like he isn't really there." The majority of what Emma said could have been easily explained by the stress Benji felt after Grandpa's death, but his mind kept going back to the mention of the song. His stomach sank.

"We need to do something," was all Gideon could muster as he got out of bed. He looked up to see Wyatt rubbing his eyes in the doorway. The commotion must have woken him. "I think I'm going to call Agatha and Miles and see what they think." He reached for his phone on the nightstand and proceeded to make the calls. Miles was quick to say he would be over in a minute. Gideon knew that would be the easy call.

As the phone rang, he held his breath. A tired-sounding Agatha said, "What do you want?"

"Agatha, it's happening again, but this time it's my Uncle." There was a long pause. "Are you there?"

"So now it matters?"

"I'm sorry?"

"So, now that it personally affects you, it matters."

"Listen, I don't have time to argue about this…"

"No, of course, you don't because someone you care about is in a life-or-death situation. You were perfectly willing to let anyone else in this town suffer for 'the greater good,' but now that all has changed, hasn't it?"

"Listen! I've already lost too much as it is. I don't want to bury any more of my family! You know what, forget it!" The phone clicked as he hung up on her. He took a moment to compose himself and then turned to Emma, who was holding Wyatt by the door.

"We need to go and tell Miguel."

Miguel lay in bed feeling a combination of foolishness and terror. Foolish for how the fight had gone with Benji, who he would continue to stay mad at for how easily he fell asleep and terrified for something he could not comprehend or make sense of. His mind was a storm of thoughts that he wished would be interrupted, but when the three kids burst into the room with the lights on, he regretted thinking that. They were all breathing as if they had sprinted down the hall to get there. Miguel was first up since he never actually fell asleep, and Benji slowly and grumpily followed behind.

"What is going on?" Miguel shouted, looking back and forth between the kids for an answer.

Emma was the first to find her voice, "Uncle Benji is in danger. He's going to die!"

"He might die; I mean, if we don't do something quickly, he will," Gideon added.

Miguel said nothing but looked at the two eldest children in shock. "Nothing you are saying to me is making sense."

"There is a curse on this town, or a ritual or some fucked up thing that causes people to die."

"Language, Gideon." chimed in Benji, still half asleep.

"You are about to become her next victim," said Emma.

Benji shook his head, "Don't entertain this nonsense, Miguel. I don't know what they are doing here, but I am about to…"

Gideon interrupted. "That woman all in white, well, that thing that kind of looked like a woman I saw? It's all her doing."

Miguel felt his heart drop when he heard that, "That thing I saw." He turned to look over at Benji, who returned an irritated glance.

"You saw it, Miguel?" Gideon asked.

"Uh yeah, no, I don't know what I saw. It was pretty far away; it could have been anything."

"No. You know what you saw; it just doesn't make any sense. You need to believe us here." Gideon said. Miguel stood there facing the truth he had feared since he started noticing weird things happening in the house. For once, he was at a loss for words. Terror like this made words hard to find. The only thing that shook him out of that state was noticing Benji walking fast toward their bedroom door.

"Where are you going?" Miguel asked

"Away from all this. I just can't take any more of it!" Benji charged past the kids, carefully avoiding Wyatt, who was in the doorway. Miguel and everyone else followed him downstairs.

"Benji, please, we should hear them out," Miguel shouted after him.

"Benji turned at the base of the stairs. "Do you hear how crazy you sound? This place has turned all of you insane."

"We saw the ritual. We know the symptoms," Gideon shot back."

"And I know the symptoms of mass hysteria, so I'm going to sleep downstairs in the sane part of the manor. You all can stay upstairs with your fantasies." Benji turned toward the front door as he heard the sound of a car pulling in. "Oh, who the hell is that?" Benji swung open the doors and walked outside. Everyone else followed to find Agatha pulling in with Miles in the passenger seat of her car.

"Why are they here?" Benji shouted.

"They are here to help; they know about it, too," Gideon shouted back.

"What is in the drinking water here?" Benji yelled as he walked away from the house toward the woodline. Miguel noticed that this caused the kids to run after him in a panic.

"Uncle Benji, please don't go there," Emma yelled after him. Agatha and Miles joined them as well. Miguel just followed, feeling unsure how to take everything that was happening.

"Mr. Kavanagh, you have to listen. This is some crazy sci-fi stuff here, but it's all real," Miles yelled. Benji shook his head and kept walking. When he reached the woodline, he stopped, turned around, and took a moment to look at everyone surrounding him with worried eyes. Miguel wanted to take him back inside to bed. He just wanted all of this to stop happening. Everyone fell silent, and Benji took a deep breath before speaking.

"Since day one, I have done all I could to make a new life for us. I knew it wasn't going to be easy, but I was determined to try. I felt that as long as my partner had my back and my nephews and niece kept a good attitude about it all, we could get through anything. But this is just far beyond the scope of what I can handle. None of you wanted this to work. All of you have done everything to make our lives here impossible. However, to drum up some nonsense about a monster? It's pathetic." Tears formed in his eyes. "I'm not my brother. He and I could not be more different, but I truly wanted to do right by him. Now my father's dead, and I have a family so determined to make this fail they would gaslight me into believing, seriously believing, that I'm to become a victim in some CULTISH MAGIC RITUAL." At that, Benji's arms fell to his sides, his eyes glossed over, and he looked as though he was zapped of all his energy. Without another word, he turned around and began marching into the woods.

"Benji? Where are you going? Benji!" Miguel yelled. There was a gasp from someone else as shock rippled through their small group. Gideon's mind raced. He had to find a way to fix this, but how? He glanced over to see Benji nearing the trees. Miguel and Emma took off behind him.

"We have to call the mayor," Miles said.

"We can't do that. She wants this to happen, remember?" Agatha replied.

Miles glanced nervously over to Benji. "What do we do then?" Agatha was right. The mayor would never help them. He felt the pit in his stomach grow wider. Then he remembered something.

"Find me." He started pacing back and forth while everyone watched.

"Are you okay?" Miles asked.

Gideon looked over Miles's shoulder and noticed Wyatt crying under the statue of the woman. "Find me," he said under his breath, suddenly rushing over toward the woods.

"Where are you going?" Agatha called behind him.

"We need shovels. We have to find it," Gideon said, looking back. He noticed their confused expressions and turned around. "Look, we need to find the emerald bracelet to break the curse. I think this house, or maybe the woman, was trying to show me that."

"Okay, so do we have to dig for it somewhere?" Miles asked.

"No, not just somewhere. Right here. I believe it is right under that statue of the weeping woman."

In the distance, he heard Miguel's cries and then the high-pitched scream that came from Emma. "We need those shovels right now," said Gideon.

⋆

Emma wrapped her arms around Benji's leg like a boa constrictor while digging her feet into the ground. She ignored the pain throbbing through her ankle as Benji seemed to still be able to lift his legs with ease as if her effort amounted to nothing. Miguel was shouting and trying to reason with his partner despite Emma already knowing that he was too far gone to understand. Emma's arms grew exhausted, but she gripped as tight as she could in the hope that something would come from her effort.

Gideon and Agatha were able to find two decent shovels in a small shed near the garden, while Miles got stuck with an old metal rake. "But how do you know it's here? How can you be so sure?"

"I'm not, okay? I am just going on what she showed me. I don't have any other ideas," Gideon replied as he broke ground under the statue. They all worked together to dig a hole in front of the weeping statue. Miles, despite his limitations, was able to dig a surprising amount of dirt out of the hole.

"So we dig up this body, right?" Miles asked between every toss of earth out of their way.

"Yes," Gideon and Agatha said at the same time.

"Okay." Miles threw a few shovels of dirt out before continuing. "Okay, but what are we doing with the body afterward? Are we burning it? Smashing it? Is Gideon going to give it a true lover's kiss?"

"Just dig Miles. We will come up with something when we get there," Gideon said, stopping to wipe sweat from his brow. He looked up, noticing they had gotten a few feet deep already, but time was not on their side, so without another moment's rest, he returned to digging.

***

Emma felt a sharp pain as her ankle was pulled on by a root that Benji stepped carefully over. Her grip on his leg was released, and she fell with her back on the ground. Through the pain in her legs and arms, she saw Miguel had abandoned trying to talk to Benji and started pulling on his right arm to no avail. Her breathing continued to be labored as she turned over to lift herself up. She felt helpless as tears began flowing down her cheeks.

"Please, please, not now," she said, as her heart continued to leap out of her chest and the familiar smells and sounds of the city returned to her mind. She closed her eyes in an attempt to push them out, but when she opened them, the headlights were there, racing toward her, and her mother was looking at her.

"Stop," Emma screamed as she braced for impact. Her whole body rippled as she was flung into the air, and pieces of glass and streaks of red floated by her. She could feel herself slipping.

"Come back!" The sudden shout came from somewhere she couldn't tell.

"Come back with me, please!" Miguel's voice vibrated in Emma's ears. She began to recognize things weren't right. She remembered she was not in that car. That car was destroyed. She was not with her parents; she would never be with them again. She raised her head, but every movement felt like gravity was a hundred times stronger. She moved her fingers, felt the ground, and realized she was not floating. She was not lost; she knew exactly where she was. More tears streamed down her face as she lifted her torso and slowly got to her knees. Miguel's voice was becoming more distant. She knew she needed to break free and find them. She took one big breath and, gripping the grass in her hands, she screamed, shaking whatever was making her feel heavy off, then standing back up and charging to catch up to them.

***

Gideon's vision blurred, and he stopped for a moment to rub the sweat from his eyes. He was nearly chest-deep in soil. The smell of damp earth engulfed the area, and when he looked down, he noticed small droplets of blood. He held his burning hands up to see that they were cracked and bleeding.

"I don't think there is anything here," Miles panted. He leaned back against the wall of dirt and tilted his face to the sky. "I can't breathe."

"If you're talking, you're breathing," Gideon said.

Miles glared at him. "Fine. I feel like I can't breathe."

Agatha leaned her shovel to the side. "Look at your hands."

"I'm fine. We have to keep digging. She has to be here." Agatha frowned, taking a step back.

A heaviness settled on Gideon's chest, and tears swelled behind his eyes. The woman in white had to be under the statue, for Benji's sake, he thought. He snatched the end of the shovel up and began thrusting it into the dirt, ignoring the pain that vibrated through his hands. Out of the corner of his eye, he saw Agatha attempt to reach for him. She probably wanted to comfort him, but he didn't need comforting; he didn't have time for that. That's when the end of his shovel hit something hard, and his heart lurched in his chest. "Oh my god," Agatha whispered, gaping down at the sliver of wood peeking through the dirt. "You found it."

"Help me uncover it," Gideon said, bending down to scoop dirt from the wood. They worked on uncovering it for what felt like an eternity before enough dirt was removed to allow them to open the coffin. The coffin, from what he could see, was worn, a pale resemblance of the once shiny dark wood it had been. There were intricate carvings along the sides and top, swirling and weaving through one another. He brushed his blood-stained fingers across them. There was something so familiar about the designs.

"Alright," Miles said, scrambling to get out of the hole they had dug. "I'm not being here when you open it."

Gideon didn't respond. Instead, he nodded at Agatha. They took in deep breaths and together heaved open the coffin lid. There, against yellowed lace fabric that he was sure was once a bright white, were brittle pieces of bone. He wasn't sure what he expected, but this felt more sad than disgusting to him. That's when he noticed the delicate emerald bracelet. His mind flashed to the old picture that he found in Wyatt's room. This had to be the woman in it. He frowned, reaching out and slipping the bracelet from a tiny piece of bone.

"Oh, God, you're touching it," Miles mumbled from above and made a gagging sound.

"What is that?" Agatha asked. She leaned closer for a better look. Gideon couldn't answer her. His eyes were fixed on the seemingly glowing green stones. A wave of sorrow hit Gideon, and he wasn't sure how he knew what he was supposed to do. However, before he could think about it another moment, he raised his hand and smashed the bracelet against the coffin. Agatha gasped next to him as several stones popped out of the now-broken bracelet.

***

Miguel pushed with everything he had on the chest of his husband, who was moving only slightly slower toward death. Benji was walking into the hands of a crazy-looking monster that stood in front of some giant rocks. Every time he looked back, he could see more details of the strange woman-like creature and her bright red eyes. His feet were getting dragged through the dirt, and he found it harder and harder to anchor himself.

"Come on, Benji! Wake up!" Benji continued to be unresponsive. Miguel felt hopeless until he looked down and saw Emma grab onto a leg and pull it as her own feet began to slide. At the sight of that little girl trying, Miguel refused to give up. Somehow, he knew that every moment counted and that even though the combined effort of both of them was only making the zombified Benji move a fraction slower, it had to be enough. Miguel looked back to see that the creature was only feet away from them, now standing in the same position. He was unsure what he could do to stop her if she decided to run at him.

"Stop it, you ragged bitch. Stop it now," Miguel shouted, though the creature seemed unaffected. He turned around and pushed his back into Benji, screaming as his body hurt, trying to hold him back. The banshee lifted her left hand up, showing an emerald green bracelet as she looked to be reaching out to them. A fingertip was almost able to touch the side of Miguel's face before a bright flash came from the bracelet. The light was quick, and when it was done, the bracelet had vanished. Benji stopped in place. Miguel stood up, not letting his eyes leave the creature. But she only looked down at her now naked arm, then once more at Miguel, and suddenly, for the briefest of moments, Miguel could see past the monster and at the face of what looked like a normal young woman. But before he could fully understand what he was seeing, a blinding bright light took its place, and the banshee vanished, leaving them all. Miguel turned to see a confused Benji blinking and looking around.

"Why is Emma squeezing the life out of my leg, and where are we, Peanut?"

Miguel didn't speak, instead moving to embrace him, crying heavily into his chest. With only moments to spare, Benji was saved.

Chapter 35

Gideon sat on the steps of the manor with his hands over his mouth, something he often did when he was nervous. It was dawn, and the sun was creeping up slowly. To his right, Agatha kept her gaze toward the woodline. To his left was a sleeping Wyatt. Miles, on the other hand, felt it would be smart to use music to guide Emma and the others back, assuming that it would work and they all survived. The music blared on and did little to make Gideon feel less anxious as he waited.

"Oh my god," Agatha exclaimed, causing Gideon to look up and turn toward the woods. Far to the right of the manor, he could see the silhouettes of Miguel and Benji finding their way out. Benji had Emma in his arms. Gideon jumped up at the sight and sprinted to meet them. He gave Miguel a huge hug.

"What took you guys so long?" Gideon asked.

"You try and traverse this crazy forest with minimal light," Miguel answered. "Thank you, Miles; you can turn that awful music off forever now," he yelled over Gideon's shoulder. Benji still seemed shaken by the whole ordeal.

"Hey, Uncle Benji, are you feeling better?"

"Yeah, this town is magic. It's cursed, and we are going to sell this damn house," Benji said, then began walking away. He stopped and turned around, shifting the sleeping Emma onto his shoulder. "Thank you, Gideon. You are as brave as your dad." Benji turned back around and walked toward the manor.

Gideon noticed a second car had pulled up. A frown formed on his face when he remembered that it was owned by Mayor Spruce. Both Miguel and Gideon ran up to the front of the manor to meet her. Benji was already standing in front of her with a tired Emma raising her head. "Mayor Spruce, what has you up at this early hour?" Benji asked as he let Emma down to stand on her own. The Mayor stood there for a moment, seemingly looking everywhere but at them.

As Gideon approached, he smiled and asked cheerfully, "Is something the matter, mayor?" Her face was scrunched up more than usual. She seemed to be having trouble finding the right words to say or yell. Gideon exchanged looks with everyone who knew the mayor's true identity. They all seemed to share the same nervousness, waiting to see how she might react.

"You broke the seal."

"I'm sorry?" Benji said.

"Those kids of yours broke the damn seal," She yelled, losing her composure.

"Mayor Spruce, I don't know what this is all about, but..." Miguel started, but she interrupted

"No, no, no. I want explanations. We had an understanding. We worked this all out. Do you even know what this has caused!"

"It was going to kill our uncle," Emma yelled back.

Spruce looked at several faces to confirm the truth of this, then threw down her arms and started screaming in the Gaelic language she had spoken before. She kicked the dirt before taking a breath and regaining herself, "Fine. Fine, fine, fine." She paced around for a second. "That was an impossible choice. Of course, Leath." As she yelled Mr. Leath's name, he suddenly appeared by her car, which Gideon found strange since the vehicle had seemed empty moments before.

"Deidre! What's the matter, old girl? You look unwell," Leath said as he walked over to them.

"Grab Collins. Begin the search. The seal has been broken, and we have a lot to do."

"Oh, oh, this is bad. Hmm." He turned around and walked back toward the cars.

"Listen, I am not going to mince words here," the mayor said to Gideon and the rest of the group in a calmer tone. Gideon realized that Leath had vanished again, "I'm upset. I'm upset because a lot of work went into protecting what you all just undid. I'm not going to stay angry about that now, though, because this town and all of its residents are in grave danger."

"Well, we will be out of your hair soon enough, mayor. I'll sell you this manor today if you'd like."

She let out a sharp laugh, "I don't want this old, cursed thing anymore, Mr. Kavanagh. This is not over." With that, she turned around and got in her car. Gideon stood there a while as the rest went inside to see Agatha and Miles off.

"I'm glad we could save your uncle," Agatha said, grabbing Gideon's arm.

"I'm sorry about your dad," Gideon returned, watching Agatha's eyes turn sad.

"You weren't around when that happened, but at least we stopped this from happening ever again." Gideon watched as Agatha drove off.

Then he turned to head inside before stopping cold. There, in front of him, stood a young woman dressed in white. She looked just like the woman from the picture. Her skin glowed softly, and her smile was warm and welcoming.

"You freed me; I thank you for that." Her voice came out in a whisper.

"Oh, you're welcome," Gideon responded, surprised and unsure of what to say.

"Your family is in great peril." At that, she began to fade and said one word before vanishing: "Caorthannach."

Gideon looked up, taking in a deep breath before walking into the manor.

Chapter 36

"This damned headache." Mary sat in the dark of her small living room. She couldn't remember if it was a nightmare that woke her up or some loud sound. Since the death of her last hospice care patient, Emory, she had been suffering from nightmares of being locked somewhere and not being able to escape. Tonight was especially bad. She kept her eyes closed until she noticed the lights turned on in the living room. Opening her eyes, she saw a startled Agatha at the door.

"Agi, what are you doing up so early?"

"Oh, I went to check on the Kavanaghs," Agatha replied.

Mary's headache worsened as she tried to carry on with the conversation. "Okay, fine, just head to your room for a bit?"

"Alright, Mom. Are you okay?"

"Yes, dear, just give me a moment."

Agatha walked away, and Mary went over and turned off the light in the living room again. It did little to help her throbbing head, so she walked into the kitchen to make herself a cup of hot cocoa. Afterward, she sat down, lit her favorite apple spice candle, and closed her eyes. *Ding dong.* Mary sprung awake. It was still dark in the living room, and she realized the candle had burned out. The holder was full of wax. Next to it, her once hot coco was cold. Confused, she stood and went to answer the door.

"Trick or treat!" A small pirate with an eye patch and a heavy bag of candy smiled up at her.

"Oh… I'm sorry, I don't have any candy ready."

"Lame," he yelled and ran back toward his dad. Mary shut the door and rested her back against it.

"You deserve so much better, my darling." The voice at first sounded feminine but strangely seemed to get deeper toward the end.

"Who is there?"

"Don't be afraid, Mary. All is well now; I'm here with you again." The voice of her husband brought Mary to tears, though she still felt fearful of what was happening.

"I don't understand. Where are you, Robert?"

"I'm closer than you realize, and I'm here to protect you now."

"Protect me? From who?"

"The Kavanaghs"